The Fear of Stones

Macmillan Caribbean Writers

The Fear of Stones

KEI MILLER

MACMILLAN CARIBBEAN

Macmillan Education
Between Towns Road, Oxford OX4 3PP
A division of Macmillan Publishers Limited
Companies and representatives throughout the world

www.macmillan-caribbean.com

ISBN-13: 987-1-4050-6637-2
ISBN-10: 1-4050-6637-7

Typeset by EXPO Holdings
Cover illustration by Tim Gravestock
Cover design by Tim Gravestock and Karen Thorson Hamer

Author's acknowledgements
"Tolston Closing" was first published in *Bearing Witness 3*. "The Shaman's
Prayer" first appeared in *Caribbean Writer* Volume 17, and "Calabash,
Broken" in Volume 18. "Read Out Sunday" was published in *CAPE
Communication Studies*, a textbook for "A" Level students. "Shoes for the
Dead" appeared in *Caribbean Beat*, "The Fear of Stones" in *The King's
English*, "This Dance" in *Blithe House Quarterly*.

Printed and bound in Thailand
2010 2009 2008 2007 2006
10 9 8 7 6 5 4 3 2 1

Series Preface

Writing in an easy, colloquial style, spoken in a range of voices, Kei Miller is a poet who tells stories the way an impressionist paints, in brief but vivid strokes, surely building a rhythmic accumulation of detail to form an illuminating picture. But the pictures in his challenging collection, *The Fear of Stones*, are not pretty, and few are comfortable. Drawing on an essentially Caribbean magical realism, the stories embrace obeah and the supernatural to illuminate the lives of those failed by society, the harsh influences that have shaped the spiritually maimed and the different, the misunderstandings of the outcasts' efforts for self-preservation and the grace to be themselves. It is Miller's genius as narrator that he is able to persuade the reader into sharing his own sympathy for each one of his unfortunates.

The Macmillan Caribbean Writers Series (MCW) is an exciting new collection of fine writing which treats the broad range of the Caribbean experience. The series offers a varied selection of novels and short stories, and also embraces works of non-fiction, poetry anthologies and collections of plays particularly suitable for arts and drama festivals.

As well as reviving well-loved West Indian classics and presenting new writing by established authors, MCW is proud to introduce work by newly discovered writers, such as the exceptional Miller, Martina Altmann, Deryck Bernard, Garfield Ellis, Joanne C Hillhouse, Margaret Knight and Graeme Knott. Writers on the list come from around the region, including Guyana, Trinidad, Tobago, Barbados, St Vincent, Bequia, Grenada, St Lucia, Dominica, Montserrat, Antigua, the Bahamas, Jamaica and Belize.

MCW was launched in 2003 at the Caribbean's premier literary event, the Calabash Festival in Jamaica. Macmillan Caribbean is also proud to be associated with the work of the Cropper Foundation in Trinidad, developing the talents of the region's most promising emerging writers, many of whom are contributors to MCW.

Judy Stone
Series Editor
Macmillan Caribbean Writers

The Macmillan Caribbean Writers Series

edited by Judy Stone

Non-fiction:

... and the Sirens Still Wail: *Nancy Burke*

Novels:

Jeremiah, Devil of the Woods: *Martina Altmann*
Butler, Till the Final Bell: *Michael Anthony*
For Nothing At All: *Garfield Ellis*
Such as I Have: *Garfield Ellis*
The Boy from Willow Bend: *Joanne C Hillhouse*
Dancing Nude in the Moonlight: *Joanne C Hillhouse*
Alonso and the Drug Baron: *Evan Jones*
Ginger Lily: *Margaret Knight*
Exclusion Zone: *Graeme Knott*
Brother Man: *Roger Mais*
The Humming-Bird Tree: *Ian McDonald*
There's No Place Like ... : *Tessa McWatt*
Ruler in Hiroona: *G C H Thomas*

Plays:

Champions of the Gayelle: *(ed. Judy Stone)*
  Plays by Alwin Bully, Zeno Constance & Pat Cumper
You Can Lead a Horse to Water and other plays: *(ed. Judy Stone)*
  Plays by Winston Saunders, Dennis Scott & Godfrey Sealy

Stories:

Going Home and other tales from Guyana:
  Deryck M Bernard
The Sisters and Manco's Stories: *Jan Carew*
The Fear of Stones: *Kei Miller*
The Annihilation of Fish and other stories: *Anthony C Winkler*

Author's acknowledgements

Those who taught: Funso, Merle, and especially Mervyn

Those who read and made suggestions: Richard, Adziko

Those who supported: my parents, my sister, de man dem, Ronald

Special thanks to the Cropper Foundation for the space.

Contents

Contents

Walking on the Tiger Road

Mary was a woman who knew many things. She knew how to crack eggs in basins of water, leave them overnight and then see if they took the shape of ship or coffin or anything that might signal the future. She knew howling dogs digging up the yard meant that somebody was going to die for sure. Mary knew how to read signs, so that morning when the woodpecker bored his way through, she wiped her onion hands into the floral skirt, looked skywards and whispered a prayer of thanks. It had worked out finally. Lord be praised!

For months now, she had got into the habit of watching the bird and his slow progress up there on the lightpost. It annoyed her at first, the persistent tap-tap-tapping, this bongo-rhythm that wouldn't end. Then one morning it came to her that the bird's pecking was like a prayer – like one of her specific prayers. Each morning for the past many years she would tell herself the parable of the persistent widow, then go down on her knees to make her case before the Lord again, though it seemed to her recently God's heart was made of hard wood. So she understood: the bird was a sign sent to renew her faith, and as she watched the progression – his head, then his wings, then his whole body being swallowed up in the hole he was burrowing, her heart tightened with excitement. That morning when Mary actually saw the bird break through, coming out on the other side, her heart trembled with joy and she found herself crying, whispering thanks to the Lord.

But the woodpecker paced angrily from one opening to the next, squawking loudly. Mary frowned. He had bored all the way through and what else could it mean but that her prayer had been answered – that she was going to see her son after ten long years! What could be so upsetting about that?

*

Dear Mama,

Up here, sometimes the cold get so cold it start to hurt you. That is the only bad thing. The winter. And worse than the cold is the dark. By four o'clock it stay just like midnight – you wonder where the day gone already, and why the night must last so long. And then some days walking up the street you will realize again, as if for the first time, that you actually miss seeing people skin. Black skin, red skin, white skin – it don't matter. 'Cause in the winter everybody walk round bundled up – like them in their own little houses. But that is the only bad thing, Mama. I guess is the price you pay – Lord knows I willing to pay the price.

Dear Mama,

I was in studio all day today. We was doing background vocals for this fellow they say going to be the next big thing. Mama, I sing until my throat was hurting bad bad, and after that I sing some more. It upsetting when these white guys go on like they know everything and you realize they don't know a damn. You ask "what wrong with how I sing it last time?" And they tell you: "Nothing; we just trying something different." Well, they paying me well... so I won't go on too bad. I will send you something by Western Union tomorrow. Remember to tell me if there is anything you need.

Dear Mama,

Sometimes I have this nice dream where you standing outside the gate pulling love bush off the hedges. Up the road is me that walking to see you. And you wipe the sweat out your eyes and look up to see me coming. You forget everything you was doing

*and come running towards me. And then it come in just like
the Bible story, 'cause you shout out to everybody in Grove's
Pen, "We going have party tonight. 'Cause my son who did
dead is alive again."*

Mary sighed, releasing the breath she usually held whenever
reading through some of Mark's letters. She refolded them
carefully, placed them back into the suitcase and pushed the
suitcase back under the bed. Each time she read any of his
letters it was like she was in a different world for a while.
That's where she wanted to be right now – away from the bird
that was still on the lightpole, squawking *Quaw! Quaw!* as if he
wanted the whole world to listen to him.

*

His mother once taught him how to read dreams but he had
forgotten the lessons. So it was strange. He woke up that night,
his fingers desperately wrapped around his neck because for a
moment it had seemed the tiger was real and about to rip into
his jugular. When the dream finally let him go, he whispered
to himself, *well this must mean something.*

For the ten years he had lived in America, he had thought
nothing of the messages in dreams. He saw such things as
backward, superstitious – Jamaican! His had not been a
voluntary exile and so for the first two years, forced to live in
the United States, he had found it therapeutic to lambast
everything about his native island. Even when he settled and
lost some of the cynicism, it was because his coming to terms
with the past meant suppressing most of his memories.

Perhaps then, it was because this was his first night back in
Jamaica that he could think so easily about superstition and
dream-reading, as if the island was the only place where
certain things could be thought. His return had been almost as
sudden as his exodus. The evening before, he had been

walking towards home, up 34th Street in New York, when a stone-drunk Indian man stumbled out of a bar and bounced into him. The man grabbed onto Mark's shoulder, trying to steady himself. He swayed there for a bit, thick vodka breath falling like a sour cloud over his victim.

"Y-y-y-you…" the Indian man stammered. "Y-y-you…", unable to get out whatever it was he wanted to say. Till finally, still holding on to Mark's shoulder, he almost hiccupped "Y-you faggot nigger!" then vomited over Mark's shoes.

Mark wanted to scream right there in the middle of Manhattan to everyone who had turned their eyes away, "but you see the things I have to put up with, eeh!!? You see how this drunk coolie boy take liberty with me!" He wanted to shout *Bumboclawt!* He wanted to slam the Indian man's face into the pavement. He wanted to cry. He wanted, he wanted to see his mother; his mother whom he had not seen in ten years. His mother who would never call him a faggot nigger then throw up over his brand new Aldo shoes. And that is how, without packing, with only a credit card, a driver's licence and a few dollars in his pocket, Mark stepped into the street, flagged down a taxi and headed for the airport. And in his mind, it was going to be just the way he had always dreamed it. The prodigal son returning to his mother.

So he was back in Jamaica, sleeping in a hotel room that first night before he continued on to Grove's Pen, St Thomas, to surprise Miss Mary. He had fallen asleep as soon as he entered the room, as if the dream had been there all along waiting to possess him. It reminded him of the ones he had in which he was just falling; there was that same hollow sense of danger and that complete inability to do anything about it except wake up. He had been walking on a road and more felt than saw the large tiger stalking behind him. He turned around once and watched the cat lick her lips. Trembling, he started walking faster. The cat didn't growl, she didn't bare her sharp teeth. Her yellow eyes didn't glare. She simply whipped her tail and started bounding towards him. He started to run, or at least attempted to; for some reason he couldn't go very fast. He tried to scream but the sound locked itself in his throat. He ran in slow motion, his muscles aching at their ineffectiveness. The tiger pounced on him, knocked him to the floor and rested her heavy paws on his chest.

Finally, she growled, low and terrifying. Hot saliva dribbled down onto Mark's face. The cat lifted her head to the sky and roared, the full length of each tooth making its own private threat. She lowered her face, going in for the kill; Mark struggled and somehow managed to get his fingers up around his neck in protection. *Don't kill me!* he pleaded, *please don't kill me.*

*

Is me one raise him. Is truth I telling. As soon as him daddy find out I had belly him just pick up and gone and I never see him again. But I never did look for him either. And yes, sometimes when I look back at everything, I regret it. But is how life is.

But God is good. Imagine, me alone raising a man child and him never give me no trouble! For true. The boy was an angel. Obedient, kind, polite! Everything a mother could want. And while some people a preach "If you spare de rod, you go spoil de child," I swear to you, I never had to raise the strap to him once. And him don't spoil neither! Marky never get into no fight at school – and if like I tell him "Stay in tonight," him wasn't going to back-answer. Him was happy to stay wid him mother and is like I had a friend in him.

But then, suppose you hear my Mark sing, eh? You woulda fret! Oh Jeezas. Every Sunday at church when him go up to the pulpit and open him mout', I tell you God himself would come down from heaven and listen! I see the most hard-hearted people bawl when Mark sing. Is that's how him making him big money in the States now. Him singing up there, and not for no lickle screbby people. I proud of that boy, I can't even tell you.

But Lord, why him had to walk like that – swinging the hips, him wrist dem flapping like any woman? When him was little I did used to close me eyes and pretend I don't see it, and is the worst t'ing I could do, because it grow into the boy and then everybody a whisper whisper so till even me hear:

Is like is a girl chile Miss Mary a raise!

And I feel so shame and I sorry that I keep the boy so close to me, that is me make him hate him father. But that was just the beginning. Them started saying worse, everybody was carrying the news:

Miss Mary son Mark a battyman!

Which one? The tall lanky fair colour bwoy?

Is the only one she have. Yu nuh feel seh him funny?

Fi truth. Me did always t'ink him gwaan a way.

But no! Me son is not no battyman. Him just have woman ways cause him never have no daddy fi look up to.

I make him do sixth form in Kingston, and then college, just hoping that the distance would do him some good, make him start to behave like a proper man, and to get him away from them no-good people round here who just want to destroy him, to take him down!

Lord, and him was doing so well in town, getting good grade. It break mi heart the night him come home, like him was in a fight, the poor boy bruise up! An' him tell me say, "Mama, I get caught in something. And I can't stay in Jamaica," like him want to cry, "I have to leave. Dem might even take me to jail." And then him really start cry and me start cry too. Neither of us can even speak. But I finally get the words out of mi heart, "How you could go a Kingston an' involve youself up in drugs, eh Mark? In criminal t'ings! I woulda never expec' that of you! No. Not you! You smarter than that, boy! How you could do it?"

"Mama! Is not drugs," him say, wiping 'way the tears, and for a while is almost like him want to laugh. "Jus' trus' me. I can't explain, but I have to go, Mama. I need to go away. Them will murder me out here."

So I raise the money quick quick, and put him on a plane going to Miami. No, I never understand what was going on. Mi one son, going on so shame, like him couldn't even look him own mother in the eyes. And now it break me heart every day to know that him not here. That I can't see him when I want.

But after ten years him finally coming back to me! Him coming back to see me and I glad. Oh Jeezas I glad! You can imagine?

So tell me why this blasted bird up there on the lightpost, walking from hole to hole, bawling *Look out, mother! Danger!*

*

Mark did not like documentaries, but once he sat down for two hours to watch one. It was the story of a Rastafarian from Georgetown, Guyana, who, after drumming and chanting nyabhingi for years, decided to save his every last cent so he could repatriate himself to the motherland. The day when he landed in Nigeria, he walked out of the airport, never stopping to ask for directions. He walked for five days until he finally collapsed in a village many miles out of the city. The women from the village came to him with water, wiped his face and forced him to drink. When he revived enough he started weeping uncontrollably. "What is the trouble, son?" an old woman asked. She was speaking her language of course and he, who had never heard or studied that tongue answered her fluently "I just sorry that I ever leave. I hope you can forgive me."

Forgive him! As if he or his ancestors had had some say in it, had sailed across the Atlantic willing to become slaves. Strange thoughts will take hold of a man when he returns to a place that used to be home. A guilty nostalgia overcame Mark for the whole taxi ride to St Thomas. He was smelling Jamaica again, the heat and vinyl and stale tobacco of the old, beige taxi, the specific blend of salt and almond as they drove by the St Thomas coast, the pungent sweetness of mangoes being sold on the roadside. When he stopped to buy corn soup, an old woman served it out and placed it gently in his hands. He said, "Thank you, Mums." Mums. To a woman he had never met in his life; it was just that Jamaican way of showing respect to older people, to big women who could have been your mother anyway. Mums. His face clouded over with the pain of nostalgia, like he wanted to cry right then and there; and the old woman seeing the pain on his face, bent over and asked "What is the trouble, son?" and he almost answered, "I just sorry that I ever leave."

An hour more of driving, and finally the taxi came to the weathered sign which read *Welcome to Grove's Pen.* The car turned in but Mark instructed the driver, "Stop here." The taxi stopped, the driver grimacing in confusion as real signs of community didn't begin for another half a mile. But for the sake and romance of his daydream, Mark did not want to return home in the back of a car. He wanted to walk.

He paid the taxi fare, stepped out, and many minutes after the car left, he just stood there looking around, taking it all in. He noticed, of course, that things had changed somewhat in ten years. Tarring had been done, a bit of painting, lightpoles were put up and there was some semblance of a sidewalk. But it was still the same hopelessly curvy road. There was still tell-tale sand of a beach nearby. Giant coconut trees continued to grow on either side of the road, their spindly leaves meeting in the air, so the evening sun could only come through the spaces that were left. And Mark's breath caught in terror as he looked on this effect – the coconut trees, the light, the shadows – the road as if it were striped – orange and black, orange and black.

*

In the ten years of his exile, the strong suspicion that Miss Mary's boy was gay had almost been forgotten. Of course, on the heels of his departure it had become a bona fide fact. Why had he flown out so suddenly? A scandalous story came out of Kingston and offered an explanation. It said the boy was caught in an act of "buggery" (many had to look up the word) and charges were going to be pressed.

But time passed; new stories stole the spotlight; people moved out and others moved in. The "bona fide fact" withered back down to a strong suspicion, dwindled even further to a rumour, and finally settled at being only a shady myth. If anyone brought it up in conversation, the listeners tolerated it the way we tolerate a man who swears he saw the ghost of his mother the night before: even if amused and thankful for the story, no one really believes him.

And so Idle Bwoy, who had got himself expelled from three schools and now just idled by the shop, only knew the myth. He couldn't have guessed that it was attached to the strange thin man who was making his way up the road. Idle Bwoy only observed, with much amusement, the timidity, how it was this outsider walked, looking down on the gravel as if he were suspicious of its intentions. No. Idle Bwoy had not a clue who Mark was. Not until old Mrs Pinnock came out of the shop lugging two five-pound bags of flour and a pumpkin. She stopped, squinted at the tall figure in the road, mumbling to herself, "but what a boy favour... mmmm... no... it couldn't be... but lawd God... but no..." Then the figure turned around, faced her directly, and smiled. The old woman screamed out: "*Mark!* Jeeesus! Is you? Mark Ranglin! Miss Mary boy child!"

And Idle Bwoy, who was never very sensible, who thought all his thoughts aloud never knowing what to keep to himself, grinned mischievously. He turned the bottle of Malta to his head, drained the contents, wiped his lips and asked, "So is you dem say a battyman?"

Mark's mother told him once, "When dog growl at you, try don't look scared. Him not meaning to bite you, he only want to see what you made of. Stand up straight bwoy – even when you scared don't show it. The animal will respect you and leave you alone." So somewhere inside, Mark knew how he should respond to this question. But it caught him off-guard. After ten years! Ten years? Had they been waiting on him all this time?

Idle Bwoy waited; Mark stared. *Laugh it off*, he told himself. *Give some indignant response: "A wha' di rhaatid yu a talk 'bout?"* But the sounds wouldn't come out properly. He didn't know, had never felt comfortable with the language of macho Jamaican men, with their gesticulations or their mannerisms. Mark was being asked to perform, and suddenly he had stage fright. Perhaps Idle Bwoy would have thought nothing if Mark had simply sucked his teeth and ignored him, but instead Mark walked over to the low wall where he was sitting and awkwardly rested his hand on Idle Bwoy's thigh and asked, "What kinda question that?"

*

No one really understood why Idle Bwoy had got into so many fights in high school. In second form he punched the daylights out of a tall boy named Hortence – Hortence who everyone loved because he was the star runner on the track team. The whole school was upset that Idle Bwoy had beat him up, beat him up so badly he had to be carried to the hospital. And for what reason? Hortence wasn't the kind of person to trouble anybody. So they put it down to jealousy. Idle Bwoy was just plain jealous because Hortence was bright, and popular, and good-looking.

But it wasn't that at all. Idle Bwoy was really beating up himself. Sometimes when he wasn't careful he would have some wicked thoughts; he would imagine himself and Hortence doing things that made him feel ashamed and dirty. Idle Bwoy tried hard not to think those thoughts, but one night he woke up, his heart racing, because he was having a nasty dream, and it was all about him and Hortence. The next day when he went to school and saw the handsome boy he had dreamed about, a sudden rage built up inside Idle Bwoy, and he hit Hortence hard. Then hit him again and again and again.

When Idle Bwoy shouted at Mark, "Is you dem say a battyman?" he was trying to be separate from something he knew was a part of him; he was trying to distance himself from himself. And when Mark's hand rested on his thigh, Idle Bwoy thought he had been identified; thought that in this action, a complete stranger had seen through him, and said, "Yes, we both are." Idle Bwoy panicked. The old urge to fight welled up inside. He lifted his knee and slammed his foot into Mark's chest, who screamed in pain as he fell back to the ground.

"B-b-but what is this!" Miss Pinnock, stunned and stammering, "Idle Bwoy, is I-like you have the devil in you." She was caught between reprimanding the delinquent and helping Mark up, but right then all the men from the shop ran out asking somewhat delightedly, "Is what? Is what happen?"

"Nuh dat battyman a put argument to me!" Idle Bwoy replied, "Miss Mary boy!" He flung his empty Malta bottle at

11

the man who was still struggling to stand up. "Battyman! We nuh want you here."

Trembling, Mark finally stood up, took one look at the small crowd and knew that it wouldn't make any sense trying to argue his case. He turned around, still holding his chest, and continued to walk towards his mother's house. Tears stung his eyes and he was shivering with the tension of not knowing what was happening behind him, wondering if he should run instead of walk.

Idle Bwoy picked up another stone and flung it hard into the centre of Mark's back. "Nasty man!" Mark flinched in pain. The other men picked up stones and soon they were following him home. They pelted him, searched for bigger stones along the roadside, then pelted him some more, bruising him as much as they could. It was as if each man was doing the same as Idle Bwoy, looking for his own sin, his own private world of frustration and throwing it at this scapegoat, at Miss Mary's only child.

A well-aimed stone finally opened up his skull and blood dripped into his eyes. He staggered, tried to stand up again. His clothes were torn, his shirt hanging like shreds around him. He was bleeding in many places, and there was still no intermission to the stones being thrown. They opened his cuts wider. Wider.

So he thought, *I going to die! But Lord, make me see Mama one more time. I want to tell her that I sorry. I sorry for leaving you Mama! I sorry that I used to hate you, because I never know me father. I sorry, because sometimes I did t'ink you was the cause for who I is. But I looking back at everything, and I see that you did good Mama. You did awright.*

*

Thursday evening should have found Mary in her kitchen, elbow deep in a basin of coconut trash, kneading white sugar into the mixture, adding food colouring, then dividing it into lumps so she could bake grater cakes which she would later sell. But her nerves didn't allow for such activities that evening. She was locked up in her room, on the bed, the pillow pulled tightly over her ears which still didn't block out the sound. The woodpecker, as if to spite her, decided she hadn't heard the half of what noise he could create.

The bird had started from early in the morning. *Quaw!! Quaw!! Quaw!!*

"I don't know is what you warning 'bout," she had said to him earnestly, "Please just leave me alone!" But the bird didn't let up. *Quaw! Quaw!* Everywhere she went, everything she did, *Quaw! Quaw!* She went back out screaming at him. He ignored her. *Quaw! Quaw!* And after a few hours Mary felt like her body was turned inside out, like the sound was in her veins and behind her eyelids so she could see it.

The day had wound its way down to evening and still the woodpecker hadn't rested. *Quaw! Quaw!* Mary was trembling, crying in her bed, the pillow only dulling the noise, but not able to cut it out completely.

Then suddenly she made up her mind. She was going to kill the bird. She got out of the bed, balled up her fists and walked outside picking up a stone on the way.

"Jesus God I hear you!" she screamed when she reached the lightpost. And so focused was her attention on the bird that it was only with the smallest fraction of her brain that she noticed the bloodied man staggering towards her, the crowd behind him with their stones. For a while Mary even thought they had come to help her knock down the bird. She didn't see them shamefacedly drop their missiles.

She picked up more pebbles and started throwing them up at the bird. "I tired of you!" she was shouting between breaths and stones. "Me son coming back and I don't care what you have to say 'bout that!" Pelting him but missing, not realizing the bird had finally stopped and was only looking at the crowd, looking at his prophecy. "I just sick...", tears rolling down her face, "... and tired", her body shaking, "of you and you damn quaw quaw!"

*

When the sun dipped below the horizon, it was as if it was running away from being witness to this scene: the crowd, desperate in their silence, looking at their guilty Cain-hands then to the road beneath their feet.

Mary was still stoning the bird, without stones. She grabbed fistfuls of air and hurled it up at the woodpecker who had retreated inside and buried his red head in his black plumes, as if he was suddenly cold and afraid.

Mark was not standing any more. Bleeding, he grabbed at the road before him, trying to get a grip on the gravel, trying to pull himself towards his mother, his mother who he had not seen in ten years, his mother who at that moment, the insanity draining from her eyes, turned around finally and saw him.

Tolston Closing

When Naomi woke up that early morning, outside was dark and the moon and even a few stars could still be seen. It was the seventh day of the seventh month, which meant everywhere women were giving birth to ugly babies who would grow up beautiful. Beautiful and strong and able to gloat over the ones who had called them retards, and baff-hand, and fool-fool. Naomi decided it was time for her too, to give a kind of birth. She got out of the bed and walked to the window. Later the children would remark at this. They would tell how they slept very soundly the whole night and throughout that early morning hour and how very strange that was. Every morning of the past two years their mother got out of bed early, walked to the bathroom, knelt at the toilet, her face on the seat, her long dreadlocks hanging down and floating in the bowl, and wept bitterly. Every morning. Huge choking sobs. The children would wake up resentfully, frown, then try to go back to sleep. But that morning they were not pulled from their dreams. Naomi didn't go to the bathroom. She went to the window, opened it, and said to the world *Is time I tell myself the truth*. At that instance her insides grew hard. For she had always been a soft woman. The past two years in particular. Soft and foolish.

Tolston is not God, she said. All those years she had worshipped him. Everything he said was gospel. She had believed in him.

I not stupid! she said next. Around him, she had been stupid, clumsy, awkward. But if he wasn't God then she wasn't the weakling she had always acted as.

15

The last admission proved the hardest. It didn't want to come out but Naomi forced it.

Tolston not coming back! There. It was said. He should have returned a year and a half ago. His contract had only been for six months. Do a bit of farm work, earn some much-needed money, and then come back. But he never did. Finally Naomi admitted the obvious: *him never plan to.*

A tear coursed down her face. Naomi looked across the dark morning and remembered him:

He had taken her to this place where the houses were still small but there was space and grass and a river where women washed and children played; this place where people were still poor but not angry all the time; where men didn't sulk by the shop or the corner all livelong day, but used their muscles and worked the land. It was Tolston who had taken her here, to Pascha Hills, away from the city. She was eighteen and sold oranges at the market. Tolston walked by her stall without noticing either her or her goods. He was the tallest, darkest man she had ever seen. Things were bad that day. She needed to make some sales desperately so her two younger brothers could go to school, buy lunch, and not beg on the roadside as they were growing accustomed to doing; so her father could buy liquor and not abuse her immediately; so her mother could buy make-up to hide the bruises. She called to him, "Rastafari! Ital oranges me have here a sell! Come buy from me!" He turned around and looked down, his locks falling in his face.

Naomi had to tilt her head back completely to meet his gaze and under it she suddenly felt small and ugly. The gap-toothed smile, the hazel eyes, her hair with three different colours, her face, round but small, which protested against every hairstyle she had yet tried; she hated all of these things. He liked her.

"Ital oranges," she repeated more softly, handing him one, "de sweetest you ever taste!"

He held the hand that the fruit was in. "I want you meet my mother." Just like that. He was never one to beat around the bush. She went with him that same night to Pascha Hills. They arrived late when everyone was asleep and the night was cool. She loved the place immediately – the red dirt road, all the small houses made from bamboo, the sheds outside which were kitchens, the sound of the river not-too-far off, the tall coconut trees that swayed in the night breeze.

"This is where my mother live." He pointed to a house which looked like every other.

She stopped. "We not going in?"

Tolston hesitated. "No. She old. Let we not wake her up right now." He lingered awhile. "I take care of my mada, 'cause is she bring de I in dis world. And I love her. But she don't understand me. She don't understand how I sight Rasta. She want to know why I knot up my hair. Always saying how I naw get nuh job look like dis. But she don't understand." It had never occurred to Naomi that when people were passionate about something they believed in they changed their lives, even their appearance, to suit it. Tolston seemed noble to her that night. She looked on his locks and remembered Samson from the bible story.

They continued walking. The road angled downhill and after several minutes of stubbing their toes and stepping in mushes of fallen mangos, they came to the river. The sounds of water gushing and frogs croaking were overpowering.

They sat side by side and there was no discomfort in the long periods of silence between them. "You know dis song?" Tolston asked her, before he started singing,

> *By the rivers of Babylon*
> *Where we sat down*
> *And there we wept*

17

> *As we remembered Zion*
> *But the wicked they carried us away in captivity*
> *And required from us a song*
> *But how can we sing the Lord's song*
> *In a strange land?*

It was as if he actually did remember this place called Zion, as if he possessed some wisdom that understood everything: both the history and the future of the world. It was by that river Tolston started teaching Naomi about Babylon, the place they lived in. How it was black people were poor in Jamaica because it wasn't their natural home. How they were stolen from a greater country, from Zion, and transplanted here, to a destiny of poverty. But there were worse Babylons, Tolston told her. Places where black people were few, and they weren't allowed to remember Zion. Like in America, and England, Tolston told her. No Rastafari or Revivalism or even Pocomania. A worse and lonely Babylon, Tolston said. Naomi loved him.

Much later he squeezed her hand, "Nobody going to hear us down here." Just like that. He was never one to beat around the bush. She helped him unzip his pants and he helped her with her skirt. She lay on the cool river stones, he entered her, she held him and looked at the dark sky, which slowly shifted to morning.

*

Tolston not coming back! Naomi repeated, for remembering him in those days made her miss him terribly. Those had been the good times. Then came the children. It wasn't that she regretted having them. It wasn't as if things would have been good without them. But children bring change fast.

The first time she had become pregnant, Tolston was happy. He said it was right for a rasta king and queen to have little princes and princesses. He went to the river and got more bamboo and wicker, bought two bags of cement and went to work adding to the house. Every night when they went to bed, Tolston put his ear against his wife's belly and sang to the child.

When she was seven months pregnant and very much showing, Naomi for the first time wondered what they would call the child. For three days she silently pondered it. Her father's name was Selvon and though he was a drunkard who had abused his whole family, she knew it was a fashionable thing to name children after their grandfathers or grandmothers. And then wouldn't it be great, Naomi thought, if the child were a girl, for both her own mother and Tolston's were named Mary. She decided these were good names for the child and went to Tolston with it one day while he was eating.

"Tol, I feel we should be t'inking of a name for de baby." He looked up from his food and grunted some form of agreement. She continued, "I was t'inking it would be nice, you know, if is a boy, to name him Selvon, after me daddy. And I t'ink if is a girl we..."

She stopped cold. He was glaring at her. His eyes spoke an incredible anger, and she knew the look. It was the first time she had seen it on Tolston, but she knew it well. Her own father had glared at her mother and her the same way a million times, when his brain was full of liquor and somehow he was convinced that they were nasty bitches, whores, the worst kind of women on the face of the earth. Tolston was giving her the same look now and if he was a man like her father he would begin hitting her soon. But Tolston wasn't like that and he knew how to keep his anger in check. Still, Naomi felt stupid and afraid. She cowered.

"Is foolishness like dat make Babylon prosper." It was the harshest thing he said. After that, he tried to explain his position coolly. "Listen, Naomi. I want my children have something of Africa in dem names. See how everybody walking round wid name like Sophia and Thomas and Drew. Those names are not ours. Dem don't belong to us. Dem come from Babylon. Is part of the shitstem dat keep us down. We so shame and frighten of everyt'ing dat come from de modderland, we don't want to look, or talk or dress like true black people. Nobody in dis blasted place know who dey are. Is dat keep us downpressed. I don't want dat for my pickney, Naomi. I want to give dem back dem real names. And I thought by now you woulda sight the same reasoning."

Naomi nodded. He continued, "I want show you another thing. Look how when anybody call out my name, Tolston, my picture form clear clear in your head. Me broad nose. How I tall and mawga. Don't? You t'ink of everyt'ing dat I can do good, like play guitar and how I love football. You t'ink of de t'ings I can't do to save me life. Everyt'ing 'bout me, you t'ink when you hear I name. A name is a man spirit and him soul. It fit him like a glove. But I want you know, most times is de man dat take de shape of his name. Is a t'ing to be careful wid, what you call your children."

*

These are the children of Tolston and Naomi. Kokayi, which means "He shall summon the people". At the time of the boy's birth, Tolston was reading about the prophet Marcus Mosiah Garvey. He remembered a scripture that said prophecy was one of the higher gifts and so he wanted his own son to be blessed with it. Their second son was Gowon. He was supposed to have another name, but he was born on September 12, 1988, the day Hurricane Gilbert hit Jamaica. No one could hear Naomi's screams as she bore the pains of labour, because outside was filled with the sounds of thunder and rain and wind. So the boy was given the name Gowon, which meant "Rainmaker". Their first daughter was Abeo, "Her birth brings happiness", which wasn't at all true in this case. Perhaps Tolston was trying to convince himself, but another child meant he had to work harder, sweat more, eat less, make more sacrifice. Tolston who had never worn a condom, who had said it was a Babylon tool, went to the pharmacy and timidly asked for a box of Trojans. He wore them when he remembered, but he rarely did. The fourth child was Rajabu, because he was born in July. Their fifth, a girl, was Isingu. It meant nothing, just a combination of vowels and consonants Tolston had flung together. He had sighted a new reasoning. He said the world was so completely fucked-up there was no turning back, no reclaiming of the past. He said the world needed to start afresh. Do everything afresh. Give new names and new meanings. But he never came up with a meaning for Isingu. He just drew the name out of the blue, and then went back to complaining about how tight things were.

When Naomi became pregnant for her sixth child, Tolston walked out and never came back for two days. He stunk of liquor when he returned. He told Naomi he would apply for the farm work programme and things would be all right. He left for America. The child was born and for the first time Naomi was faced with the problem of coming up with a name. Tolston had always done it. She borrowed a book from a friend and found the name Abidemi which means "Born during father's absence". Abidemi only lived a week. Perhaps the child felt her mother's depression. Perhaps she couldn't cope with that coldness, that lack of love, and so she died. Naomi cried bitterly at the funeral. But all her tears were for Tolston. She had never been without him for so long.

*

21

Two years! Two years of waiting and waiting, telling herself she could never survive without him, while doing just that. The irony of it hit her now. The people from Pascha Hills had grown tired of her tears after only a few months. Instead of a soothing word or a hug, they would say, "Lawd God you is a big woman Miss Naomi! How you mus' take things so hard?" They didn't understand. She met him when she was eighteen, a young girl who lived under her father's roof. Now she was thirty-six! Over thirty years of always living under a man's care! How was she not to feel alone and scared? Besides all that, she had given Tolston his Rasta children, his princes and princesses. And yes, things were really hard, but he was not a man without a backbone. He knew that black people had to suffer and struggle in this place. He had always known. He was the kind of man that stuck by in hard times. But now he had gone for good. What warning signals had she been given? How could she have prepared herself? How could she not grieve terribly? Naomi closed the window. *Two years!* she thought. She wouldn't wait any more. He wasn't coming back.

She walked across the room to a table where a sharp knife was kept, most often used to peel oranges. She picked it up and rested the broad side of the blade against her cheek. She remembered the time, just a few months ago, when she danced.

Ras Jacob, Tolston's good friend, had come to the house to take her out. "A Nyabinghi happening up at Nine-Miles," he told her. "I going and plenty idren go be dere. Come sister. I know you need it." So she went with him.

Ras Jacob had to park his old delivery van a good half mile away. The road after was rocky and narrow. Jacob and Naomi slowly made their way up. It was almost half an hour later when the trees opened to a large clearing. Hundreds of men and women wearing dreadlocks milled around, eating food or singing to the drums. The five drummers were under a shed, working up a sweat.

Naomi felt the sensation immediately. Some call it the old Negro feeling – a burning in the blood, a dull throbbing in the hollow below the ribs, as if the whole being was drawing into its centre; the same thing that comes upon church people when there is a sudden quiet and the pastor whispers *Jeeeeeezus!* and the old women throw their hands in the air and start rattling off in tongues. The feeling that comes when black people worship.

Ras Jacob walked off to greet some of his friends and didn't even realize or much care that Naomi had stopped walking with him. She stayed rooted in one spot, people dancing and singing around her. She looked intently on the drummers. What pain was it inside that made them beat the drums so fiercely? And how amazing, that the drums responded and spoke that pain eloquently. She watched them, sweat pouring off their dark skins, their concentration furious, their hands rapidly lifting and falling back on the goat-skinned instruments. *Bum-du-bum-dum-dum!* The people were chanting a song which they had been singing when she walked in and very likely would be singing non-stop for another hour as long as the spirit held them. But she didn't hear the words. The only thing that occupied her head was the *Bum-du-bum-dum-dum!* She began dancing. She tilted her head back, flashed her locks and moved her feet. These drummers knew her pain and they were playing it for her. She was dipping and jumping and twirling and the people around noticed, noticed how pure and spirited her movements were, and they tried to dance to her lead. *Bum-du-bum-dum-dum!* There was a poem Tolston once read to her by a Bahamian fellow. She remembered it clearly now and tears started running down her cheeks. She danced.

Bum-du-bum-dum-dum, wasn't that the sound of the ship's hold slamming shut? Bum-du-bum-dum-dum, wasn't that the sound of the casket closing? Bum-du-bum-dum-dum, wasn't that the sound of slaves banging on the ship's boards? Bum-du-bum-dum-dum, wasn't that the sound of slaves knocking on Massa's door? *Bum-du-bum-dum-dum! Bum-du-bum-dum-dum!* Naomi was jumping high and twirling, and everybody stopped trying to follow her, they just watched and nodded. Her tears were falling, flowing. *Bum-du-bum-dum-dum! Bum-du-bum-dum-dum!* Wasn't that the sound of Tolston closing the door? Wasn't that the sound of Tolston leaving? Her pain solidified into one whole, and it rose to her throat. She needed to say it, and in that spirit, in the drumming, she heard herself scream out *"Jah! Rastafari!"* The idren couldn't hold themselves back any longer. It was as if their priestess had called them. They all flashed their locks and shouted out just as she had. They started dancing again and jumping and sweating and the drummers beat on and on even into the night. But after her scream, Naomi stopped and she felt withered.

What she should have done was scream an unintelligible sound that in its rawness told everything that was in her. Instead she had formed it into something sensible and now she realized hurt and disappointment weren't things that could be expressed in precise syllables. "Jah Rastafari"? The people danced on, but didn't they see that the pain which had become solid, the pain which had risen to her throat wanting to come out, was still there? That right now, it was dissolving again and resettling in her entire being.

*

Naomi took the blade away from her face. She walked into the room where the boys slept on a grass mattress. They were beautiful children. Gowon was the one who slept the lightest and he soon opened his eyes and saw his mother there, standing with the knife in her hands. "Is what Mama?" his lips formed as he rubbed his eyes.

Naomi placed a finger against her lips even though he had made no sound to wake up the other two. "Come here," she commanded. He got up, confused, and walked to her. "Turn around." He did. She tilted his head back then held it firmly.

"Is what, Mama?"

She said nothing but he heard it, he felt it, and his heart grew instantly cold. "Mama!!!" he hissed, "Mama!!"

"Hush boy! Is all right," she said, still holding his head firmly. The knife, held close to his scalp, sawed through the dreadlocks he had been growing since he was a child. It was Tolston's rule. No razor will ever touch my children's head! But here was his mother cutting them off and for the first time he felt the morning breeze on his scalp. He cried. Naomi finished with him, and went to Kokayi. She didn't care if he slept or not, she just drew him so she could get a good angle. It was Kokayi, the eldest, who screamed when he realized what his mother was doing. *"No Mama! Mama no!!"* It was he who cried the hardest and woke all the children. Rajabu bolted up. Isingu and Abeo came running from the other room where they slept. Everything was crazy, pandemonium. The neighbours woke up wondering what was happening inside Miss Naomi's house? What the hell was going on? The children screaming and crying. But Naomi wasn't affected by any of it. Without blinking she went from one child to the next and barbered them. When she was through, giving them all their uneven, jagged hairstyles, she held her own locks and sawed through them. They felt unbelievably heavy, like they were weighing her down. Like they had always been weighing her down. She wondered how she ever stood up with them. She cut right through, till they came off in her hands, and she felt free.

Naomi glanced down on the floor, full of hair. She looked up on the children. They seemed naked, afraid, new. She did not know they were thinking the same thing of her, amazed that they hadn't seen before how tall she was, how beautiful.

"You father not coming back," she said to them, and then left the room.

Government Cows

To the Editor Madam,

It is me again, Augustus Silvera. You must be know me well by my letters. Is me who live on Parsley Lane and used to do electrician work. I write you all the while but you don't publish anything I send you so you will be glad to know, Mrs Editor, that this is the last letter you getting from me.

I don't know is what you have against me so, but before I done this whole business of buying you newspaper and sending in letter, I want you to know bout all the tings that you cause, and I hope you can sleep at night time.

First ting is Mr Norris Walcott who used to live next door to me, a tall dark gentleman who used to treat people ~~descent~~ decent. Even when the sun burning like the dickens that man would be wearing him felt hat and him take it off and nod good morning or good evening when him see you. Mr Walcott had good ways bout him, did speak proper to everybody. When him was a younger man him was the headmaster of the all-age school them now lock down on Wisherpark Avenue.

But as life go, Norris Walcott got on in years and him retire. And still, still him was willing to take the children in him house and learn them some lessons! Many evenings I sit out and listen to him teaching people pickney to read and write and telling them the history of Jamaica, bout Arawaks and Columbus and all them ~~singting~~ singthing. Him was an intelligent man, always willing to chat with you. Is plenty time I over him house slamming down dominoes with the fellows and talking bout politics. Is him first tell me "Augustus, you must write those things to the newspaper editor. Poor people can have voice in this country too."

Mrs Editor, it hurt me the day him die, and I write to you and say that we cyaant afford to bury such a good man any old way. I write the letter appealing to anyone who him did probably teach to come and help us see Mr Norris Walcott on him way to glory. Is plenty people would have helped if them did only know, but you never print the letter Mrs Editor! We dress up Norris in him good suit and felt hat but we had to put him in a simple cardboard box. Him never deserve that at all, and because of that ma'am I would like to say respectfully, I think you is a bitch!

I write you when that obeah woman, Miss Iola, move in the house up the road and every Tuesday night she disturbing the peace bout she having service. But I tell myself I could understand why for you own sake, you was afraid to print that one.

I tell you bout Sarah's big girl Lucille, who only wanted some books to study for her common entrance, cause she was a bright girl. Just some books she wanted. She never pass her common entrance and Sarah send her gone to foreign.

I did tell you bout Mrs James dog who mad and when the head take him, the dog eat all tree. I see it for myself! My own two eyes I see it. The dog was just walking and all of a sudden is like a madness fly up in him head and him start behave ignorant, and him run after Mrs James croton plant and start bite them bite them up, rip off two branches. And I write to you bout it, bout the ~~plage~~ plague of Mad Dog Disease that come to Jamaica. But I read the papers for a week and never see you put it anywhere, and if the whole of we dog population catch sick in them head, is your fault.

Mrs Editor, the last letter I write to you was bout the government cows. I don't know who tell the Priminister that the couple acres of land right across from Parsley Lane is a good place to keep that ~~heard~~ herd. Don't him know that is that same place where all the children play at day time, and where the man them play football when weekend come? Nobody did tell him that is the same piece of land that when church have crusade, them put up tent and have open air meetings? But now government decide that the cows make better use of the land than we.

The poor little boy Rayon soon get buck down by one of them government cows cause him so fool fool and don't know anyting – you always see him jumping over into the field with red shirt bout him teasing the bull, bout him see it on TV and him is matador. But one of these days the cows going kill him.

The worst thing bout it all Mrs Editor is that the stupid animal them always breaking down people fence and coming into people yard to eat down we plants. Every morning I wake up and see all six of them cramp up in front of the house and all them know how to do is to ~~shit mess~~ shit up people place like we make bathroom for them!

Listen Mrs Editor, since I not going to be writing you no more, I want you to know that though you did try your best, I still did get in you newspaper! It was when police did gun down the ole tiefing Pickaxe right in front of me house. We did all know it was going to happen one day. Even Pickaxe did know. But to see it happen, Jeesus! It still hurt. And is while them was taking up the body and I stand up there saying to meself, "Look what happen to me boy," and a reporter man come up to me and ask "You was the victim's father?" I see my opportunity and I answer yes!

The next day I was in the newspaper ma'am, and the only ting I feel sorry for was that I never remember all the tings I had to say, cause look like them would have printed it. They put in everything I did tell the reporter man. Is just that I was so choke up the day, I never said much. Just that Pickaxe was a good boy, even though him did tief in truth, him never deserve that death.

I want you to also know ma'am, that I did meet your aunty one day. The one with the coolie features who live out at

Marcus Bay, who say her husband dead from cancer ten years ago. Is me friend link me up with her because she needed some electrical tings done around the house and she couldn't afford to pay any big big money. So I went.

Is like your aunty never see man in a long long while. She was touching me here and there, always leaning on me and finally when I done the work and was ready to leave, she ask me if I could please just stay the night and keep her company cause sometimes she get scared in that big house all by herself. So I stay.

Your aunty is a sweet woman! I never do anything with her, just sit and talk and I listen. It was the next morning when a paper boy drop off the newspaper and when she come back with it in her hand she ask if I know how is her niece is the editor. I say "Is dat so?" and she tell me, proud as any peacock, yes. She tell me how you did even live with her for a while when you was going to college and how sometimes even now you visit and stay with her. She point out the room that you sleep in, and is that time I hold her and give her what she did want all night. I take her into the same room that she show me was yours, on your own bed, and I give that old woman a ~~fu~~ work make she hold on to me back and shout out some bad words that even frighten me! I want you know that!

Finally Mrs Editor, I know that there is a God up in heaven who sees and knows all and vengeance is his and I hope that one day government will put some cows in a open lot beside your house. I pray that them will knock down your fence and come into your yard and nyam everything. And after that I want them shit up the whole place. Then you will know Mrs Editor. Then you will understand.

I am etc.
Augustus Silvera

Love in the Time of Fat

Never did-a look back
Never did-a glance
Never know him would-a tumble over
Like an avalanche.
Buju Banton

This was the room before the avalanche:
– a cuckoo clock on the wall, though the annoying bird that popped out on every hour didn't look like a cuckoo at all but rather some strange abomination between a humming bird and an owl. The woman had joked about this the first time she entered the man's room and at precisely 5 pm the thing had frightened her to the point of screaming; he had laughed, told her that's how all the birds in Guadeloupe looked. She said, what a strange place to buy a cuckoo clock, in the Caribbean! And he said, yes, in fact that was the very reason he bought it. In another year, she would remember this as a reason she had loved him, that gypsy quality which could not be measured in his kinky hair or his sleepy eyes but that was there if you only got to know him.
– there were fifteen paintings ignominiously stacked between the wall and a folded ironing board. Each one was by a different artist and didn't really look like the next, but you could discern by the group of them his preference for dull colours and safety; there was nothing daring about these paintings – waterfalls and meadows and old people; safe choices. They were unmounted because he had only moved into this apartment four months ago and as it is with bachelors, he was taking long to settle in.

- there were at least seven dirty cups in the room. The air-conditioning unit didn't work and he was in the dual habit of having a cup of ice nearby and never clearing up or washing until it was desperately necessary.

- the closet door was open, revealing the kind of functional neatness typical in men who live by themselves, as if the clothes had been beaten into submission but were crossing their fingers anticipating some impending chaos, like schoolchildren right before the bell.

- there was the phone in the shape of a woman, partly hidden by a shirt tossed over it; there were the stacks of CDs beside the CD player that didn't work; there was a stack of *National Geographic* magazines right beside a few photo albums that chronicled his days at Camperdown High School, at University of the West Indies, then his three years studying and working in Baltimore. He came back to Jamaica with a digital camera so his life for the last four years was not in any album, but on his computer.

- and of course there was the bed, a large king-size bed with black covers that wasn't at all a sensible choice for the present August heat. She was sitting a little bit away from him, shaking and taking deep breaths. He was holding her wrist tightly and Jackie wasn't sure any more what had started the avalanche. Was it the cuckoo clock that had rolled into the fifteen paintings, into the seven cups, into the closet of clothes, into the phone and magazines and CDs that all seemed to tower above her right now? No, she decided. It must have been his kisses: because they had started the way avalanches do, slow at first, then building and building.

Though they had known each other for years, tonight had been their first official date. They had just come in from a play, found their way to the edge of his bed where they sat and did the requisite breathy post-mortem of the show. Then finally he kissed her. Then kissed her again and again. She arched her neck back and he pressed in closer. She felt for his hardness, unzipped him and he pulled back and started unbuttoning the top of her blouse. That's when she spun around and slapped him away with such force he fell back on the bed. Tony grabbed her by the wrist angrily, shouted "What de hell you just do that for?" but then he seemed to take a breath, relax his grip slightly, and asked her, "Jackie, what's the problem?"

But the question still felt large, as if it was going to roll over her and squash her to death. And in truth, the only answer that sprang to her head, the truthful answer, made her feel quite awkward. How could she tell him it was the light? She probably could manage being naked in front of him, but only in the dark, only with him not seeing her, seeing how fat she was.

"Jackie, I said what's the problem?"

So she thought to herself, *Yes, this is where everything going to mash up!*

*

The day Jackie lived on the edge was a Monday.

Her small blue hatchback pulled into the office early. She had not slept well the night before. Too much adrenaline in the system. She counted exactly two hundred and thirty six sheep before realizing the old trick wasn't working. After that she was only lying still, her eyes closed. Jackie saw the tell-tale orange from behind her eyelids when the day started to brighten. She heard the first bird sing. So she arrived early for work, an uncommon choice of parking spaces spread out before her. She had on her navy blue pants suit, the one which made people ask, whenever she wore it, "You losing weight there, Jackie?" And she would lie, "Yes."

Jackie was sitting at her desk by 7.30, her files for the big meeting that would begin in only a few hours opened up, and on looking over the details she found, unfortunately, that everything was in place. The mayor had confirmed. She had called all the other community leaders. The food was ordered. There were twenty-four chairs set out in the conference room and more around the corner just in case. The agenda was typed out and copied, so were the handouts. All of this was unfortunate because Jackie was the sort that needed always to be doing something, to be fixing something, to be lugging her impressive weight about the place to make sure some disaster did not happen.

In the absence of a thing to do, she suddenly found herself standing, taking a deep breath, unable to avoid a peculiar sensation that had been lurking inside her for as long as she could remember knowing herself, that feeling of being at the edge of something and not wanting to look down, of balancing on a thin piece of ground, trying desperately not to slide.

Other workers arrived. Computers, fax machines, coffee pots and photocopiers were switched on creating that symphony of white noise which is the anthem of office productivity. Jackie got up from her desk. She walked to the conference room, counted all twenty-four chairs twice. Walked back to her office, turned around, went to the cooler, sipped some water. Went back to the conference room and counted the chairs all over again. Back in her office, the phone rang. She grabbed it up. "Hello. Community Development Office."

"Is Ms March in?" A civil servant's voice, that mixture of boredom, inefficiency and strained subservience.

"Yes, Jacqueline March speaking."

"I'm calling from the Mayor's office..."

"Uh-huh..."

"Yes, His Excellency is very sorry but he won't be able to come to that one o'clock meeting you having there..."

"Excuse me?"

"He said I should tell you he has another very pressing engagement in Ocho Rios."

Jackie tried to hold on to reality but it escaped her fingers like water. She stood up, folder in one hand, the phone in the other, unable to stop the words in her head from coming out.

"Why you don't just be honest about it, eeh? Why you don't just tell me, the mayor don't give a rat's ass about community development; the mayor is a blasted poppyshow, a figurehead who don't give a damn about poor people who take time off from their own lives to come and meet with him; that bastard mayor would prefer going to Ocho Rios to gallivant with him choice whore of the month than do him fucking job!"

Jackie did not hear the stunned woman gasp. What she heard was when her office door opened and she looked up to see her supervisor, Mr Fredericks, who asked pleasantly, "How is that meeting for today coming?" And right then, it was as if Jackie had looked down the precipice, because her breath left her. *What happen? Why you make us come all the way down here for nothing? Where is the mayor? Why you wasting our time?* She could hear the questions being asked at least twenty-four times, and there was no way to stop this disaster.

The last thing to fall was Jackie, all two hundred and thirty pounds of her. Bam! A dead weight causing the whole office building to shake. And before that, the phone had fallen from her hands, the secretary still on the line hoping to hear something as juicy as the first ranting. But the first thing that fell was Jackie's folder. It simply eased its way out from her numb fingers, opened like a butterfly, and a hundred loose pages filled the air, spinning in the wind of the overhead ceiling fan, as if each one were a stone rolling downhill, before finally collapsing on the floor.

*

There should be space in every story where readers are permitted to ask questions. This is such a space.

What happened to Jackie after she fainted?

There are some things not even I know. For instance, I am not sure how she got up off the floor, whether indeed Mr Fredericks became so freaked out by the possibility that the woman had just up and died right in front of him that he stooped down and slapped and slapped her until she finally revived, her left cheek paining her for the rest of the day. Or perhaps the other story is true, that he just screamed in the doorway until other members of the staff rushed in, including one old woman who had smelling salts in her purse. I'm not certain either how she left the office, if she drove or took a taxi. But I do know she left within half an hour and headed straight for her grandmother's house in Red Hills, sat out on the verandah overlooking the mountainside that sloped eight hundred feet down to the city, and it was here, for the rest of the morning, that Jackie contemplated suicide.

But why would she want to kill herself just because she had a bad day at work?

Because that day was the proverbial straw that breaks the camel's back; it was hurt stacked upon a lifetime of hurt; depression stacked upon depression.

So what is the root of it all?

That isn't an easy question. She thought she was depressed because she was fat, because every day some stranger reminded her of the fact by calling out "Fatty! Fatty-bumbum!" Because when she drove her car over traffic humps the bottom scraped. Because every two years her clothes stopped fitting her. She was depressed because she was fat, but

36

then, there was an even deeper root to all of this. Something she had forgotten.

What about Tony, the man she was kissing?

I haven't been telling this story in a chronological way, though everything which has gone so far happened in a single day. But for now, Tony was only a friend. A very good friend. A man she met four years ago because they always sat beside each other on jazz nights at Indigo Café. They grew comfortable like this, the ritual of a glass of red wine, sipping it for the whole night and passing comments about whichever band or performer was on stage. They began talking on the phone, and then they knew each other's birthday, you know, that slow, determined process which becomes good friendship. And that's what he was now, and that is all. A very good friend. The kind who without a second thought takes over the gear stick when you get a call while driving; the kind who is allowed to call your mother "that bitch!", because he understands sometimes you need to call her that but you can't, so he does it for you; the kind whose apartment you go to when you're really upset and you don't want to talk about it, you just want to be, and possibly to scream, and he won't ask you anything, he will just be, beside you holding your hand, simply being. So yes, Jackie was in love with Tony, but she didn't know that yet.

But... but... how could she not know she was in love?

Because everything must find its own beginning. And again, it was because she was fat. It was because in her final year of university she fell in love with a man named Michael. Crazy love. She started collecting pinecones and seashells and wearing hibiscuses in her hair, perfume in her bosom. Each time his hand brushed against hers she ran home to write poems. Then one night she just blurted it out. They were drinking hot chocolate, or maybe it was just coffee – who can remember the little details, like where the light was coming from? Maybe the moon was shining. But the radio... the radio was definitely playing a Nat King Cole song, a voice crooning something so romantic it made Jackie sigh and look over into Michael's eyes and say, "I'm so in love with you, you know that?" And he froze. Stiff – solid – comatose – unmoving. Ice. Frozen so much Jackie felt the chill coming from him. She called his name five times to no response, and then she said sorry five times, but still it didn't break the spell. And she looked on his face and could see not only shock, but beneath it something of disgust. So she got up and ran away, the tears unstoppable, and when she had reached a good distance and turned back to look, he was still sitting there, frozen. You ask *how could she not know she was in love?* Easy! She had been in love at least four times but the feeling was never returned. Her heart had been crushed under the avalanche of disinterest, so Jackie didn't pay attention to it any more. Oftentimes, she did not know how she felt other than depressed.

But look at this! We have exhausted the space reserved for questions and have reached the middle of our story. As it is with avalanches, it all goes downhill from here. If you must stop to take a breath, now is a good time.

*

Life is the sum of weird events. Sometimes we never know what things are happening in a precise way at a precise time to shape our lives. Take for instance your conception – that final climactic thrust which sent one of your halves rushing to meet its other – if that had been done at a slightly different angle, perhaps in another moment, sooner or later, you would be a different person altogether – different features, different experiences. In truth, you wouldn't be you. And tell me what is more random, more unpredictable, than the position in which a man achieves his orgasm? Yet this too is added in the equation, in the sum of what amounts to life and history and the world.

They will tell you if Napoleon Bonaparte, in that most crucial moment of the Battle of Waterloo, had not suddenly come down with a bout of the shits, then he would have triumphed. What would have happened then to the New World? To the Caribbean? To Kingston, Jamaica, where our story takes place? It wouldn't have been the same sorry set of English planters and imported Africans and indentured Asians all brought here to mix up and blend up and finally give birth to me – me, existing in that ethereal place narrators do. Nor would there have been any Tony, or any Jackie who we now meet again, sitting down on that same piece of Red Hills ground overlooking the city.

In a way she was really looking inward, trying to make sense of things and wondering how the events of her life could add up to this depression. She was counting up everything and found it still didn't balance. So she thought, "Is like I forget something important." Forgotten! Gone out of her mind completely! Like a song she used to sing in church: Never-to-be-remembered-any-moooore. And this frustration – an amnesiac who cannot recall her name or place in the world – made her look out, not to New Port East where the cranes look like giant metal giraffes, but beyond that. The courage was growing inside to be done with it, once and for all. She closed her eyes and swayed there, feeling the pull of the valley below.

But life is the miraculous sum of weird events. What happened next must have been divine intervention or perhaps the author's invention (I've decided they are the same thing), but as Jackie built up the nerve to throw herself off the cliff, her cellular phone rang and it was Tony.

He had been trying to call her for an hour, couldn't get through. But, as if her desperation had sent out its own signal and called him to her, when Tony tried once again, her phone rang. When she answered all he could hear himself saying was "Jackie! Jackie! Jackie, is that you?" his voice trembling, full of relief and concern and triumph. Relief because he was finally hearing her voice. He had called the office and heard that she wasn't well; it had taken an hour to get through to her. Concern because he still didn't know how she was doing. And triumph, because he was a man in love – and here she was, maiden in distress, so probably this time he could prove himself the knight in shining armour, maybe this time he could win her love.

"Jackie! Jackie! Jackie, is that you?"

"Yes Tony. Is me," she said, breathing heavily, because his voice had just pulled her from the edge.

In those strange silent seconds in which the two of them only breathed and panicked and felt overwhelmed by their individual heartbeats, it must have all been said. It must have. Because when he opened his mouth again, it was only to say, "There's a play on tonight." And she said "Yes!" in an all too dramatic way, as if he had proposed to her. A tear was running down her face. And he, with equal solemnity and awkwardness, said, "Thank you. I guess I'll pick you up around eight."

"Yeah. Around eight. That's good."

"Okay."

"Okay then."

"Yeah."

"Yeah man."

Jackie put down the phone, and a schoolgirl's giggle bubbled up from out of her heart.

She sat down in the grass, looked towards the city, looked down the mountain where she had almost flung herself, and suddenly remembered Lovers' Leap. The story goes, two slave lovers threw themselves off, preferring to die than be separated. Jackie had visited the site once and the reality of the place had surprised her. When she imagined the story she saw the lovers simply jumping off a bluff, straight down into the sea. But Lovers' Leap wasn't a bluff, it was a jagged cliff sloping downward, so if two people jumped, they would hit levels of sharp rock all the way down, their bones breaking over and over again. They would have died long before reaching the sea, and would have together become one big red ball of broken flesh, an over-ripe apple, bearing witness to this: *if love is the seed that starts the avalanche, then the fruit of love is death.*

*

We must return to the room where I began this story. Tony still holding on to Jackie's wrist and the same ominous question filling the room: *Jackie, I said what's the problem?*

And then there was guilt. Tony's guilt, because suddenly he thought he understood. He slid off the bed, down on his knees, gently holding Jackie's hand and said, "Sorry! I'm sorry, baby. I don't know why we going so fast. We have all the time in the world. We doing this thing too quick."

She couldn't hold back any longer. It came out in one strangled scream, "Is because I too fat, Tony! I too fat. Don't pretend you don't see it. O God I don't even know what you feel 'bout me. I don't know if you... if... if you love... O God! I just can't do this!"

He stepped back from her at that moment, hurt. The thing he almost said was, "You not fat at all!" But that wasn't true. The actual truth was right then welling up in his heart and if he had found a way to put words to it, it would have sounded something like, "It don't matter, Jackie! Just like I know you don't count all o' my imperfections. Our love is beyond that kind of foolishness." But he was a man who understood sometimes words weren't helpful, sometimes you need to just be. So he sat back on the bed, drew her to his chest and just

41

held her, allowing her words to shape the silence around them.

For almost two hours they sat like that, two hours in which she finally understood that he loved her. Actually loved her without compromise. So she whispered, "Make love to me."

"You sure?"

She tilted her head and kissed him. He began again to unbutton her blouse.

Tony would never understand that in this simple act of undressing, he was not so much releasing her from her blouse as he was, finally, releasing something else.

*

Here is the thing that Jackie had forgotten: the sky in 1987, when she was eighteen and skinny. She forgot how it was so much bluer then and how you walked around with pieces of it in your bones. If you looked closely at any of the dance moves of the day, you would see they were all attempts to fly. So what she remembered as Tony unbuttoned her blouse was that in 1987 she had been growing wings.

That's why, one Tuesday midday, she began walking the one-mile distance to Sharon Mott's house. Sharon had called her up, breathy with the news of a party the night before: how absolutely fabulous it was, how John Peterson had been there and had gone on the dance floor and taught them all a brand new move, how it was such a pity that she, Jackie, had missed out but if she didn't want to come over right away and learn it (as well as hear all the other suss) because it was summer and Sharon didn't want her best friend to be left too far behind. So Jackie pulled on her purple corduroy skirt, just above the knees, a big white T-shirt and a jeans jacket despite the sun, and she left her house, walking that walk with sky in the bones, on her way to learn a new way to fly.

Jackie remembered whistling on the way to Sharon's house. It was just that kind of day, that bebop kind of feeling, so the footsteps behind her were an interruption to the tune she had been walking to. She might not have been frightened ordinarily. It was midday and Lilith Avenue was popular, so it was bound to have other people walking on it. No, she might not have been frightened, but the sound was like the smell of the gully behind her house. The gully with its stagnant water, dead pets and over-ripe fruits that had fallen from mango and soursop trees hanging over it, a deep, musky, choking smell – that's what it was, coming towards her as footsteps.

She didn't scream when he grabbed her; in a way she was not surprised. He pulled her into an empty lot surrounded by zinc fencing and if she could have arranged her thoughts in that terrible moment, she would have reflected, *Is so this world evil for true!* But she could not arrange thoughts, or words, or her breath or even a scream. She was trembling and numb at the same time. The rag crusted with cement, which he stuffed into her mouth to keep her silent was not necessary.

He was younger than she was, a boy working at one of the nearby construction sites. He seemed frightened and did it quickly. Pulled her skirt down, unzipped himself and after a few thrusts it was over and he was running away.

She lay there, the taste of concrete in her mouth, the smell of stagnant water, dead cats and rotten soursop in her nose, sky bleeding from her bones. She lay there as if she might never get up again, waiting for the world to swallow her. The sun had already set, the moon was shining and travelling across the sky when Jackie got up, brushed down her skirt with an absent kind of sadness and walked zombie-like back to her house.

Her father accosted her when she stepped in. "Where you been all day, eh!?"

She looked at him blankly, only aware of the need to bathe and a terrible, terrible hunger inside her. "Any food left for me?"

*

Now this was the room under the avalanche:
- a cuckoo clock on the wall.
- clothes on the floor.
- Tony's lips on Jackie's breasts, his feet excitedly tapping the floor; her eyes flung open and full of sudden. Sudden memory, sudden knowledge, the sudden smell of gully in her nose. It made her lose perspective. She became certain of all the wrong things. Like she was certain it was 1987; certain she was being held in an open lot surrounded by zinc fencing; certain the man presently sucking her nipples was a young construction worker she had never met before in her life.

And life... life is the sum of strange events. Did I say this already? That from the minute we are conceived, moments are rolling into each other, gaining speed, taking us into the next moment? And sometimes you will meet someone else in this roll downhill – which is all life really is – and all of your moments become intertwined with this other person's moments and it becomes one big red ball.

And gullies. Jackie does not like the choked smell of gullies. The smell of a rapist's footsteps. And she does not like the zinc rising all around her, making her feel trapped.

And Tony is whispering, "I love you, I love you."

But sometimes a word alone, the vibration of it, can loosen a stone from where it held itself on top a snow mountain – and you know what happens when the stone trembles and is released.

And Jackie, who is certain of every wrong thing, is thinking, *Is so this world evil for true.* Because now, fifteen years later, she is able to arrange her thoughts, and her words, and her breath.

There is no rule that says a girl must learn she cannot fly.

And there are the fifteen paintings and the seven cups and Guadeloupe and the black covers, and the room like a hungry ocean waiting for a ball of broken flesh to fall into it, the avalanche to end.

Tony is whispering, "I want you."

Jackie is arranging herself to scream.

The Shaman's Prayer

Rem basti dome feru den catar
rem basti dome gehtin catar-im.
A chant for rain

Barefoot and shirtless, Samuel made his way up to the big house as the sun yawned itself awake behind him. He swung the white bucket from arm to arm as each one quickly grew tired of the weight. The morning's catch still fluttered, fighting for oxygen and plotting a way back to the ocean. Samuel glanced down into the muddied water and on the five snappers. He grinned, wondering in his slightly twisted fourteen-year-old-boy way, was it possible for fish to drown?

She was looking on him; he could sense it without lifting his eyes to the balcony of the big grey house, intrusive and predatory in the village. "So the bitch come back!" he whispered to himself on behalf of every jack man and woman who lived in Hoberson, who would want to say it themselves, but who would have lost their tongues on the very news of her arrival, much less on the sight of her. They were braver when she was gone, of course. Passing Irene on the veranda, they would call out, "The bitch still in foreign? Is a long time she gone man!"

"The devil's work take a hell of a time to do," Irene would answer, and they would laugh knowingly, nervously.

But Samuel, for all his bravery, didn't share the view of "every jack man and woman in Hoberson." He didn't mind how she would stare at him. He had grown up in the big house and he understood that her interest was not sinister. It was just her strange way to look intently, unashamedly on anything that grabbed her interest. It was as if anything worth looking at was worth more than a glance. Samuel lifted his head and his eyes met hers, and for a while they stared at each other, comfortably, woman and boy. He was no fool; he knew that she was evil, "evil" in the way that his mother and the pastor described the word: she didn't go to church or believe in Jesus, she made no effort to be polite to anyone, she smoked! Occasionally, she used the word "fuck". Samuel knew she was evil but wasn't sure, any more, that being evil was such a bad thing.

The sun started to burn his back and he realized he had been standing there for a while. He continued plodding towards the house with the bucket and all at once he thought to himself: *if anyone knows how to drown fish, she will.*

*

The silence in the big house was constant. Constant in the way the owner was not. It stayed there all year; she would leave for long periods without telling anyone. Just like that. Irene would realize, probably on the fourth day, that the boss had neither been seen nor heard from, and this realization having hit home would produce such a sourness, such an immensity of bitterness in the housekeeper, that everyone stayed far from her that day. Irene would go about the house furiously muttering, cruelly weeding and pruning the houseplants, yanking off old leaves as if they were cancers, speaking her anger in a cacophony of pots.

In the night she would tremble, anoint herself with oil and rock herself to sleep. "That obeah woman can't pay me enough to do this, I swear. She can't pay me!" But in the morning, Irene was ready to do that most loathsome task: climb the stairs, push open the master bedroom door, go all the way into that dark bedroom with its purple curtains, go over to the dresser and pick up the envelope of money that had been left there on purpose. For in these times of absence,

Irene was in charge of the house: of paying the gardener and herself, of fetching the electrician or plumber if need be, of buying groceries, of being mistress to the silence.

The silence in the big house was constant, yet it changed complexions; and now that the owner was back, it had become something darker. With an earthquake moving about inside her, Irene went about her kitchen duties viciously, upset that she had to fry eggs in olive oil and make it so that the yolk was still runny (*nasty!*), that she had to boil tea with mango root (*after is not no horse I making tonic for!*), that she had to put petals of hibiscus on the toast (*but see ya dear God!*). She hatefully placed the items on a tray and was ready to turn her foul temper towards Samuel who hadn't come back yet, but just at that moment he pushed the door open, allowing the smell of fish and his sweat to pour in. She sucked her teeth.

"Is snapper you get there?"

"That's what you tell me to get."

She looked in the bucket. "*Hmph*. Well, see her food dere. Please you just take it and give her now."

Samuel put down the bucket and picked up the tray of food. "And I need you back down here!" she warned.

He disappeared, leaving his mother in the silence.

*

Rem basti dome feru den catar, rem basti dome gehtin catar-im. The woman who had been staring at Samuel was still on the patio, and so caught up in repeating the words, she never heard when he pushed the door open and walked in. Only when he put the tray of food on the dresser, and the glass and plates tinkled, did she turn slightly and notice his presence. He lowered himself into the plush purple carpet, pulled his feet into a Yoga position and waited. She turned back and went on chanting, *rem basti dome feru den catar. Rem basti dome gehtin catar-im.*

But the words were hollow now. She was busy exploring the frightening possibility that she might have actually missed Samuel, that there might be space in her heart to carry some sort of sentiment for someone who lived in Hoberson. His sitting back there was exactly what she liked about him – the fact that he had never been afraid of her, that he had a backbone; that he could look her directly in the eyes. So she stopped and called to him, "Don't stay there in the dark."

He stood up, went out to the balcony and, despite two strong wicker chairs, eased his way back to the floor, his eyes widening at the panoramic view of zinc roof tops, of the thin road playing hide and seek between mango trees, of the ocean further out with its blinding reflection of the sun, of the beach with its old boats and nets and dark, muscled fishermen sorting through the morning's catch. She followed his gaze and wondered if he would be surprised at how small the fishermen appeared from up here, if he would under-stand why, in the arrogance of such scenery, one might look at them as insects, something to be stepped on and squashed.

"Is what that you was singing a while ago?" he asked suddenly. "Is obeah?"

"No."

"Then what?"

She was silent. He waited. "It's something to make rain fall. I learned it when I was away."

"Is who teach you?"

"A kind of Indian they call a shaman."

"That sound like obeah," he said stubbornly.

They were silent.

"You want to learn it?" He thought about this for only a second before nodding. She taught him the words and then standing side by side, they looked out on the blue day with its white clouds: *rem basti dome feru den catar, rem basti dome gehtin catar-im,* over and over.

"But how come nothing not happening?" he complained when his throat was dry.

She sat on one of the chairs and looked on the beach and the fishermen, "Because it's not natural yet. Every new language is like this, you have to say it a million times, roll it over your tongue until you're comfortable with it, and then you can tap into the magic."

Samuel held on to the railing and shouted, *"Rem basti dome feru den catar! Rem basti dome gehtin catar-im!"*

But the sky remained a nurse uniform blue, perfect camouflage to the thunder bulging behind it.

*

Irene was so angry by the time he came back down, she shook with the effort to suppress her words. *Why the hell you stay up there so long! Don't you know it dangerous to hang 'round she for any length of time? Don't you have sense!?* But then, it was she herself who had sent him up, and it pained her to know she would have to send him again. So what could she really say? Irene was angry and fully intent on taking it out on this last snapper twitching on the counter. She raised the rolling pin, ready to club it dead but Samuel dashed to the counter, swiped the fish away from danger and begged, "Please Mama, make me just keep this one" and without waiting for an answer, ran outside to deliver the fish back into the white bucket of salt water.

The housekeeper was stunned into further silence. She felt her blood burning her insides and muttered nonsensical things to herself.

Samuel returned.

Irene walked over stiffly with the four fish and a knife, "I don't know what get into you, but you just get these fish ready right now, and please be careful with that knife!"

"I know how to use a stupid knife."

"Don't back answer me today boy! Jesus help me, don't think you so big I can't lace you backside, you hear! And you had better learn this lesson from now – don't you ever get so confident in anything that you going to feel that nothing can happen to you. 'Me know how to use a knife'! Eh! Who de raas you think you is? Devon down de road do carpentry for twenty years when him cut off him big finger! Or you forget Joe-Joe? Him could climb coconut tree with him eyes close, and one day you see how him drop out de tree and kill himself! Don't get so damn boasty 'bout what you can do, boy. Learn that! The day when fish kiss him teeth at the ocean, is the same day him go drown in it!"

*

Asha's Restaurant and Disco was a modest establishment with a thatch roof and walls that had never advanced from their concrete-block and cement beginnings. The "Disco" was really Miss Asha's fancy CD player on which she was forever playing a selection of Aretha Franklin's greatest hits. The restaurant catered to the occasional eco-tourist who wandered in from the nearby Treasure Beach area, but on the night the woman who owned the big house returned it was April and there were hardly any of those white patrons around.

Three fishermen were playing an uneven game of dominoes under a street light. Miss Asha, a big-breasted Indian woman with an oily bandana tied around her head, was sitting on the front steps when Irene passed by. She called out, "Irene. Heh. You under fire now. I hear that you boss come back."

"Lawd," Irene sighed, a sound like coconut trees falling, "don't even talk it. This life have enough stress as it is. If you ever know the t'ings that woman have me doing. Eh!"

"Mmmm," Miss Asha made the sound deep in her chest, shaking her head in disapproval. "And from somebody like she who grow up in this community."

The three domino players and Irene groaned together. "Lawd Miss Asha, not this again!" one of the men complained.

"But is the truth! Is here she born! Right here in Hoberson. I remember."

"Yes, yes," Irene continued mockingly, "and she did have a black mother."

"Yes. Black black black. She is not full white. Her name was Lisa and she did quiet and keep to herself, just like you see her now. But then you can imagine this fair-skin pickney when she start to grow breast and get shape and all them things, her brown hair long down into her back. Woi! She was driving the man them mad. Heh. And you know how it is man love a girl who give him a challenge. And that's why one of them old fellows hold her down one day. And is not no laughing matter," Asha said glaring at one of the domino players who had begun to snicker. "The man decide say him go deal with her case and same so him a kiss her up and take off her clothes. She don't bat an eye, she don't even make a sound, just lay down same so like a dead smaddy, just a look 'pon him …"

"But is like you was there, Asha," Jacob smiled.

"No man! Is the man feel how something was too strange 'bout it after a while. Like him doing a thing wid her, but she just cold and naw say nothing and is so him start to feel like ice was forming inside him and him get up and run 'way! Yes. Get so frighten that him run and tell everybody that him see, even him wife! Man all beg her to draw a bath with hot water to melt the ice inside him.

But listen, same time him trying to get warm, is the same time him sweating like the dickens. All pus was running down him body and him say how him feel so cold inside. Just cold, cold, cold. And the same evening him dead!

I not sure exactly what happen after that. I know the little girl Lisa had to leave but the mother did stay – Irene and Jacob supposed to remember her – a old woman name Miss Johnson and she did live on the same piece of land where that witch build her house now. Miss Johnson live there until she old and dead and them bury her right there.

And remember when this lady here come, she mash down the house and mash down the gravestone. Oh Lord! An' dat's why we know she was involve in obeah – how you can do dat to somebody gravestone just so? Eh. But she do it, and build up dat big castle. And I tell you is she same one! Is Miss Johnson same daughter come back! Same little brown girl who used to name Lisa."

There was a long moment of silence until finally Irene chuckled. "I hear you tell dat same story already Asha, and you know is why I too can't believe you...? Lisa! You believe say that obeah woman could have a pretty name like Lisa?" Irene laughed exaggeratedly but then stopped and said almost to herself, "But you know that is over sixteen years I working in that house, sixteen years, and that woman don't tell me her name even once."

*

She was on the balcony again. *Rem basti dome feru den catar! Rem basti dome gehtin catar-im!* The words soft on her tongue now, intoned differently. *Rem basti dome feru den catar! Rem basti dome gehtin catar-im!* Growing familiar. *Rem basti dome feru den catar! Rem basti dome gehtin catar-im!* Easy... natural.

She was trying to keep her calm, to focus on the words alone. But at the same time she was wondering, why this blasted rain don't fall already, eh?

*

53

Samuel was in his secret place behind the big house, somewhere in the orchard of prickly orange trees. He hid in the shadows of this mini-forest because, though the rooms at this side of the house were unoccupied, they still seemed to stare down accusingly at him. He would have felt awkward if anyone were to suddenly come up on him and witness this experiment: his hand, more than elbow deep in the white bucket, holding the fish down at the bottom.

Samuel was in his secret place because he was avoiding the company of those other children from Hoberson. His mother would never admit it, would never own up to the gratitude she was supposed to be filled with, but her generous salary from working at the big house had afforded her son school books; the silence of the mansion had given him space to study and now he was going to Munro College while every other child from the community went to St Michael's Technical, if indeed they went to high school at all. So Samuel didn't like them, because he felt that they were dull, and also, because they were black.

His own blackness did not deter him from such prejudice. How many times had his mother told him about his father, how he was a light-skinned Indian man with bright eyes and straight hair and all of that. The fact that Samuel was as dark and African as they came was only a matter of inconvenience. It meant for him, he could not show on the outside what he was on the inside: something lighter, something more distinguished, something beautiful, something like his mother's boss.

In a surprise move, the fish twitched violently and escaped the prison of Samuel's hands, tearing the skin of the boy's palm with its bony dorsal fins. Samuel screamed and sank the bleeding hand in the dirt beside him.

"Blasted fish! I going to fix you case. Just watch."

*

The prayer was being repeated mechanically, her lips and tongue forming the words on their own accord: *Rem basti dome feru den catar, rem basti dome gehtin catar-im.* Easy now. So easy, like the perfect key sliding into the groove of its lock. She was slurring the words, drifting in and out of consciousness, sometimes sleeping right there, on her feet.

She was angry when this happened and would bolt straight up. She hated that after all these years she would only have to close her eyes to see it all over again – this man, this big black man stinking of fish, holding on to her twelve-year-old self. She remembered his hard penis as purple, and she could still feel it, bruising its way inside her, and him, between each thrust, asking the same question over and over, "Why you so quiet, eeh?", as if her silence made her deserve this, "Why you so quiet?", sweating on her, "Why you so quiet?", she wanting to throw up, "Why you so quiet, you don't like it?"

And all she could think as she stared at him stonily was, "Die! Die now!"

But at this point, what did she care about all that, she berated herself. What did she care about village matters? She did not. All she cared about now was rain. She wanted the sky to open and an ocean to fall out of it. And maybe if it fell hard enough, the world would be destroyed again. And yes, if everyone drowned, she didn't much care about that either.

Rem basti dome feru den catar, rem basti dome gehtin catar-im! Thunder pealed across the sky and she felt it deep in her stomach. She held on to her belly and stumbled into the room, falling on the bed. Another clap of thunder sounded and she tore off her panties and spread her legs wide.

Rem basti dome feru den catar! Rem basti dome gehtin catar-im! And the sky, its womb swollen with rain, gritted its teeth and pushed out.

*

The old people stricken with arthritis were confused. Their bones tightened painfully with the promise of rain and yet they were looking outside on a perfectly blue Tuesday. How could they have known then, that it *was* about to rain, but that all the dark clouds had converged and confined themselves to a single ceiling, a single bedroom? How could they have even guessed that right now, sheet lightning flashed across that specific room, brightening its purple interior, lifting strange shadows from out of its corners? How could they suspect that it had already started to drizzle; that a woman was in the midst of all this, lying on her bed, unconscious to everything happening around her, her lips repeating, repeating, repeating the shaman's prayer.

*

The fishermen screamed and the collective sound travelled all the way down to Treasure Beach.

The countryside paused, holding its breath in fear. The sound did not seem to belong to grown men, but rather some schoolgirls whose admirers in their warped shows of affection had dropped a frog down their uniforms. But it had been composed of too many voices; it had been too loud, too terrified! So the people in their houses who had no clue of what was happening outside, fumbled over themselves making the signs of the cross and babbled hasty prayers trying to invite Jesus into their hearts as Pastor had admonished them to do each Sunday; they were not certain any more if the Second Coming was announced by a trumpet or by the terrifying screams they had just heard.

Most of the fishermen on the boats and on the beach were also caught up invoking some form of divine protection, Pentecostal style. Others merely lowered themselves in their boats or in the sand, and shivered. Who had ever seen something like this? What else could it mean but judgement, but evil! The ocean had all of a sudden started flashing spots of silver.

It was fish. Thousands and thousands of fish of all sizes, jumping straight out of the water, their gills splayed, their mouths open wide as if they had been drowning and needed desperately to come up for air.

*

For a few minutes, he couldn't move. The screams – the fish – the lightning – it had happened one right after the other and Samuel was left in a state of confusion, immobile.

He had given up on his experiment and was about to exact his revenge on the snapper. He had planned to dip into the bucket, grab the fish, impale it on one of the sharpest spines of the orange trees, and then leave it there, crucified. But then came the screams from the ocean – blood curdling screams – and Samuel felt his own blood run cold. He turned around instinctively to look, though all he could see was the broad backside of the big house.

And then the snapper leapt straight out of the bucket, straight up into the air, landed by the orange tree roots, and seemed to gratefully suck down gulps of air.

And then the big house brightened as if lightning was moving about inside it, and then a huge thunder – ear-splitting thunder – and he heard what must have been all the glass in the house break.

And then it was the sound of water – water like a hundred showers had been turned on – water like Dunns River Falls, coming from inside the house. And then it was his mother screaming Psalm 23, screaming the Lord's Prayer, screaming a combination of the two. And so for a few minutes, Samuel could not move.

Finally his muscles released him and he was sprinting towards the house, his heart feeling as though it was lodged in his windpipe and pounding with every roar of thunder and every scream his mother made. What the hell was happening in there? Was anything wrong with his mother, or worse, was anything wrong with the woman upstairs? He fumbled over the backdoor knob, finally got it open and stepped into the rolling thunder, the soaked carpet, the sound of rain beating down, the sound of Irene in some corner not so much screaming any more as she was crying. He headed for the stairs.

"Samuel! Samuel!" His mother grabbed on to him from behind, buried her face in his back and wept. "You see how dat woman evil for true. You see what happening? Jesus Christ. She can't pay me enough for this Samuel. Nobody can pay me enough for this!"

He made his mother hold him right there; he allowed her to continue crying, because it felt right. But he was listening to the storm upstairs, to the thunder and the sizzling lightning. It took all of his strength not to shout at her, *MAMA! Let me go!* He wanted so badly to run up there and save the woman – to save her from drowning.

Read Out Sunday

This is how Sue gave her life to God and got back her virginity.

That Sunday was church as usual. The same women as always in Jesus hats, their hands raised and their eyes squeezed so tightly shut as if by sheer willpower they were going to transfigure themselves out of Satan's clutches and into the arms of the Saviour. These were the kinds of women whose lives were in constant peril – always having to spin themselves out of the reach of demons, always walking with a bottle of olive oil ready to sprinkle it on the heads of imaginary serpents. But when Pastor Desmond climbed up on the pulpit, it was not the ever present danger of hell he preached, nor the vigilance one must practise to fight Lucifer and his cohorts each day. Pastor Desmond instead spoke on the miracle of forgiveness. He told them God had a great memory, but an even greater forgetter. And after God forgave, you were a sinner no more. So bad man could be made meek. And t'ief could be made honest. And for those who had fallen by the wayside (*Fallen pastor! Fallen!*), they could be made like virgins again. And so it was that Sue Moses sprang up out of her seat, bawling living eye water, ran to the altar and flung herself down. She carried on and she carried on, such a cowbawling they had never seen before at Mount Sinai Church of God. Even Sister Mabel – Sister Mabel who once called Sue the whore of Babylon (*Yu got a Jezebel spirit in yu, girl!*) – even she was moved to go up and hug Sue and lead her in prayer to the Lord.

But some people just too wretched and cannot be saved no matter what. Either that, or they too simple-minded. Because now that Sue found out sinners could be forgiven, and virginity could be restored, she proceeded to lose hers every Saturday night and restore it every Sunday morning. After all, the things Sue enjoyed most in life were church and sex, but until now she had felt she could never really have them both. Well, now she could and did, screaming in pleasure one night, and bawling in repentance the next morning.

Well, old people say every tree must bear its fruit, and what is to is must is. In fact, it was a wonder what happened next hadn't happened sooner: Sue, a perfectly healthy seventeen-year-old girl, got pregnant. Poor Sue. Simple-minded Sue. She could not understand it – how could she be a virgin and pregnant? Wasn't God supposed to restore her, erase the past, make things new? Wasn't that what Pastor promised? And even though Sue wasn't the most brilliant girl, she knew she had never heard of any virgin being pregnant...

... and that's when it came to her. Mary, the mother of Jesus! Immaculate conceptions. Sue fell down on her knees in astonishment and whispered a prayer, "Thank you, Lord. Thank you fi choosing me."

Well, Sister Mabel, who was not as unfamiliar with sin as she would have had people believe, was the first to notice the very slight rise in Sue's stomach and that motherly change in her countenance. So the older woman held back the girl one Sunday and told her, "Look, girl. Get rid of it. Drink some pepsi with a rusty nail in it. Rub green pawpaw seed 'pon yu belly. Whatever you do, get rid of it. Don't bring down shame 'pon youself."

But Sue followed her own programme, because what could be shameful in being the mother of God? Her belly grew and grew and people began to frown. It was the way Sue acted so proud that most rattled them – this girl who had never learnt how to study her feet in the presence of older people, how to bite her lips and wring her hands appropriately. Sue would look you straight in the eyes and talk and laugh like nothing was wrong. The members at Mount Sinai tried, they really tried. One sister gave this testimony, "You have some girls who spread them legs for any man!" and everybody look sideways at Sue who only lift up her hands and shout "Amen!" Pastor preached about the woman at the well, but Sue remained shameless.

Nothing left to do but to read her out. On that Sunday it was church as usual. The same women as always in Jesus hats, their hands raised and their eyes squeezed shut. Pastor Desmond climbed up to the pulpit and a collective shiver ran across the congregation. He started, "Brethren and sistren, there is an animal in this world, that I don't like."

The church responded, "Mmm!"

"I like every other animal except this one. I just don't like goats. No Sah!"

"No, Pastor!"

"Goats are the most stubbornest creatures you ever come across. You tell them to go this way, they go that way. You tell them to move and they don't budge. No brethren, I can't take them!"

"Oh no!"

"But I am here to tell you today, that we have some goats sitting amongst us..."

"Preach it!"

"Some of us too stubborn. God tell us to do things and we don't do them. Him tell us not to do other things and those are the things we do! Him tell us, 'Go and sin no more,' and we don't listen!"

"Amen!"

"Some of you in here is living in sin! But can I tell you brethren and sistren," his voice dipping, "the Lord says he shall separate the sheep from the goats. Somebody say Se-Pa-Rate!"

"Se-Pa-Rate!"

"He don't want the goats mixing up with the sheep! He wants them to Se-Pa-Rate!"

And to the church's astonishment, Sue rose up out of her seat, six months' worth of belly and all, and shouted in her squeaky voice, "Hallelujah! Tell it, Preacher! Tell it!" O what a brazen girl! What an unconscionable wretch! Pastor Desmond could think of nothing else but to shout back, "Sue Moses, you is the goat amongst us!"

The church was suddenly silent. No one responded, and the pastor shouted again, the words which were lingering in the silence, "Sue Moses, I say that you is a goat!" and Sister Mabel cleared her throat, "Tell it, Preacher. Tell it like it is."

"Sue, you is a goat living in sin, and we don't want to mix up with you no more. We want you out!"

"Out, Preacher. Out!"

"We want you ouuuttttt!"

Poor Sue. Simple-minded Sue. No room in the inn for her. But still, she had the glory of the Lord inside her and all over her face. The pastor screaming at her, telling her to leave, the whole church amen-ing behind him, and all she could think was *Forgive them Lord. They knows not what they do.*

Look, if Sue was guilty of any sin, it was the sin of enjoying a man's chest too much. Also the sin of indulging in that pleasure that starts at a woman's wet centre then spreads, eventually shooting through her entire body like a shock, causing her to sweat and gasp. And perhaps the sin of loving bun and condensed milk, and definitely the sin of being fool-fool. But Sue Moses was not disobedient, and when she got up out of her seat that Sunday and walked towards the pulpit instead of towards the door, it was not an act of rebellion, not in her head. She only wanted to prove that she would hold no one in malice, that she forgave them. She only wanted to extend her hand to Pastor Desmond, possibly kiss him on the forehead, and then leave.

But the pastor trembled behind the pulpit watching her approach. "I said out! *Out!*" She did not stop. "*Out I say!*" Now jumping, "Out!" Poor Sue. If only he would understand. Instead there he was shouting, close to tears, as if afraid. "Please girl! Leave the people of God!" But now Sue was right before him. She reached out her hand of forgiveness and Pastor Desmond could only see fingers pointing at him accusingly. He cried out sorrowfully, "All right! All right! Yes! Is me is the father. She tempted me, church! She tempted me and I was weak." He fell down and oh, such a cowbawling Mount Sinai Church of God had never seen or heard before.

Shoes for the Dead

He works with quiet and arrogant indifference, the kind you grow to survive a career looked down upon by everyone, that cold exterior which allows a prostitute not to cry any more when, in an aisle in the supermarket, she passes the man she did beastly things to and for the night before. The man is pushing a trolley beside his wife, the one who would shiver at his raw, animal needs, the one whom he loves so much he pays another woman to exorcise his demons through. The prostitute is doing something human now, buying milk and lettuce, and not even looking for a hello, or a profession of friendship, or anything from those eyes, so cold and lifeless as they look straight past her. She's learnt to stop crying now, and she looks at him with arrogant indifference, the same kind which Philip has as he applies the final touch of make-up on a corpse, pushes it back in the freezer and goes out to the front desk because the wind chimes by the door – their music so hefted with death that they never sound exactly like other chimes – have just announced the arrival of a customer.

"May I help you?" asks the mortician with the distinguished subservience of a butler.

The woman doesn't answer at once. There is something in servitude which lulls a master and prolongs commands. She is nearing fifty and the roots of her shoulder-length hair are their natural grey, which makes Philip guess correctly that she is debating the too-bright red and the too-straight chemicals and is approaching a style which reflects her age. The woman takes off her shades with a slight flick of the head, which makes her hair ripple. Putting them in her handbag, she speaks at last with a smile.

"Yes, how you doing? I've come to pay a bill and I hear there's some other things I might have to get for the body."

There is no grief in her voice; she speaks with the efficiency of one who has expected death and had budgeted two weeks vacation for when it happened. Her accent is layered with all the places she's been and lived till it's no accent at all, and Philip can barely distinguish the Jamaican which lies beneath it.

"What's the name?" The undertaker reaches below the counter for his thick hard-covered book of records. He doesn't look as he reaches; his is the reckless efficiency which knows that everything is where it should be.

"James Morrison," she says, and after a while adds, "He was really old." But Philip knows that already from her voice without grief.

With what would have been almost a flourish, had it been less formal, less staccato, Philip puts his glasses on his nose and opens the book, turns the pages slowly and then, reaching the last page of entries, runs his thumb down until he finds the name Morrison, James. He could have done it quicker, but there is dignity in a slowness which doesn't waste anybody's time, anyway.

"And he'll be here until Saturday?"

"Yes. It's a morning funeral."

"And we shall do the work on Mr Morrison. Make-up, clothes…"

"Yes, yes. Of course." The woman laughs.

"And a hearse will come for him."

"Yes."

"All right," Philip drawls, taking up his calculator, "that should be" – punching in the digits – "yes, one thousand nine hundred dollars."

The woman's face falls. Then she remembers that prices are different in Jamaica, and after she makes the conversion she realizes it's quite cheap. She laughs to herself and stores the experience, the way we collect anecdotes to tell our friends. She giggles and Philip is unsure what she finds funny. She counts out the cash from her wallet and gives it to him.

"You'll need to get me the things by Thursday. Powder, his suit and…" he pauses and inspects her for the first time consciously. Her clothes and her manner suggest she is educated, he decides at last. Not one to value superstition over plain and common decency. "… and shoes" he finally adds.

He is pleased that she nods readily to this and smiles, taking his hand, shaking it and looking into his face. "Thank you so much, sir. You don't know how much you've made this whole thing easier for us all." He's sure it isn't that much, because of her voice.

Though she has looked into his face, she won't remember it, Philip thinks. There is something too congruous between his appearance and his profession; a stereotype with his lankiness, his straight posture, his hairline receded to the middle of his head then stopped sharply like a razor, the rest of his hair neat and thin and low and grey. His appearance is so expected that it cannot imprint itself upon someone's mind, like Ms Kansas and Ms New York and Ms Delaware from last year's beauty contest.

*

When the woman reaches the family house where everyone is staying, she has two anecdotes to share about her trip to the morgue. She waits till she's settled into shorts and a T-shirt and has towelled off her make-up, put on a shelf all the layers of accents from all the places she's been and lived, the layers which stifle the Jamaican accent below. When she sits down to the meal of curried chicken and potato and yam and boiled green bananas, she tells them first of the one thousand nine hundred dollars and how her heart got cold around the edges.

And they all laugh dutifully. Then, she adds, "But stop! Den you nuh hear de real story yet!" and she tells them about the mortician who told her to buy powder, and a suit; she pauses before the punch line to make sure everyone is listening, and to deliver it with sufficient drama – "and shoes!!"

"But see-ya!" one of her sisters exclaims, before clapping her hands and laughing.

"Yes me dear," continues the woman, "shoes! Me just smile and nod and walk out. I buy de powder and I buy de suit. And is blue, 'cause you know how Dada did like blue suit. But kill me dead if me go buy him a pair of shoes!"

"Dat's right!" declares another sister.

"Nobody not looking 'pon him foot in de coffin," and then she adds the more important reason, "and Dada walk around enough when him did alive, me nuh want him walk nuh more, now dat him dead!"

With another burst of laughter, and another round of affirmations, the family agrees that the woman with the layers of accents, and the shoulder-length hair with nappy grey roots, is wise not to buy shoes.

*

Philip hears the door chimes on Wednesday morning, the ones that don't sound like other chimes because something about these mourn, like the hollow wailing of pipes. The man at the door has a package, a final wooden house about the size of a grown man. The undertaker signs for it, and on it is a simple note: *The things are inside.* There is no name attached to this message, and in his heart Philip curses the arrogance of a customer who thinks she is the only one who is to send him a coffin and things.

But he only curses inside, so his dignity remains intact until the delivery man and his underclass staff of haulers are gone. Only then does a small amount of the dignity erode. Philip knows this is from the woman with the too-straight, too-red hair. He lifts open the lid of the mahogany box, and sees a smart blue suit, folded neatly with a white shirt and a blue tie. And on top he sees a bottle of baby powder... not the kind he likes, because he prefers a brand only sold in a pharmacy below Half Way Tree which softens death, instead of making it so harsh and ghostly like all the other brands. But he doesn't care about the powder, because he's reasoned long ago that death isn't supposed to be soft. He takes out the suit and throws it in a chair, and throws the powder there too.

There is nothing else in the coffin. He gropes around the crevices of the white satin, but gives up soon, because that is no place shoes could hide. And he curses now, inside, but it shows in his flared nostrils, in his stern eyes; it shows.

He tries to convince himself that this is nothing to get angry over: the indecency, the wanton superstition of the woman and her family. He has seen it once too often, and there were people who asked him to do worse. Some families not only refused to buy shoes, but insisted that he put pins in the dead one's feet to prevent them from walking again. It happened often enough for his quiet and arrogant indifference not to fall to pieces when he heard it. The people asked him with no shame in their voices, no awkwardness in their eyes. They asked him for the service as if it were a natural thing, and that he should be schooled in the practice. And after so many years Philip has never been able to bring himself to pierce the dead. He lets the woman a half-mile down the road do it, and pays her a small sum. The woman lives in a house between large warehouses, which seems to draw all the shadows to it; a house with flags mounted all around. But when she leaves the house in her red turban she seems to take the shadows with her. She was happy to pierce feet – and dolls – with pins. And Philip couldn't watch after the first time, because she dipped the pins in olive oil sprinkled with black ashes before she stuck them in, and she hummed so low and loud that it rattled the old man. But the woman with the nappy grey roots hasn't asked Philip to pin her Dada down, she just hasn't bought shoes, and the old undertaker decides the gross indecency is nothing to get angry over.

He walks over to his safe. It is behind a not-done-too-well print of the Mona Lisa in the front of his establishment (he prefers establishment to shop, because there is something wrong in the notion of selling for the dead). The safe is unnecessary. There is nothing of value to outsiders in it, other than money whose amount doesn't warrant the effort of breaking in. But Philip values the contents; both the money and a letter for when he's gone. It's not a will, just instructions for his burial arrangements, because he wants that to go well, having seen so many go wrong in his time. In the letter he says he only wants his body viewed for half an hour, because more than that and those who have sharp noses start to smell death, and then decay. After half an hour the coffin is to be locked forever, and the pastor's words are to be short but powerful like poetry, so he only wants Rev E V Grant from Westmoreland to do it, even though he doesn't know the man personally, but he's seen him do funerals, and he is good. In the letter he asks his wife to wear black lace over her head because that looks so proper and respectable on a weeping widow. But most importantly, in the letter, he says he wants a black suit, and a bow tie, and his hat; and he wants shoes. Black English leather, the kind you can shine so bright it glares; the kind with a line of pin-sized holes which run around the whole shoe and meet at the front in a heart shape. That's what he wants most of all, and no expense is to be spared. None.

Philip locks the safe after he's retrieved two hundred dollars and walks out the store not checking anything, with that kind of reckless efficiency that knows everything is where it should be. He only puts up the misleading "Be back in 15 minutes" sign and pulls the door closed. He hums a song he's learnt to hum to the tune of the door chimes. He thinks they're the liveliest things in his store. The only thing that doesn't have death lingering on it.

He walks down the avenue passing other houses, and warehouses which throw their oppressive shadows on a flagged house perched between them. He passes women who in the early evening wear loose jeans and buttoned up shirts, and do human things... but the fall of night will see them metamorphose into bright colours and tight clothes. Philip looks past them and through them with cold lifeless eyes of no recognition, and they do the same, because they've learnt not to cry.

He walks until he comes to a woman who sells shoes and slippers that he can get for two hundred dollars or less. He realizes he didn't check the size of Morrison, James's, feet, but then he hardly does these days because he's a good estimator. So he asks for a good sturdy pair of English loafers in size eleven.

The woman searches. "We only got ten an' a half sir," she says, pushing the shoes to him, hoping to still make a sale. "I guess that will have to do" he accepts, handing her the two hundred dollars, and then waiting expectantly until she reluctantly gives him twenty dollars change.

*

The funeral for Morrison, James, came and went peacefully. Peaceful because no one opened the lower lid of the casket and brought him a complaint about the shoes; not like the time in 1968 when a pallbearer with arms weak from alcohol, which was supposed to be a balm for his grief, let go of his burden and the casket tilted and stood vertical and the lid flew open and the dead body came out, and people weren't as scared because the dead body seemed to be standing for a few seconds as they were because he was standing in shoes. The family had cussed Philip bitterly for the whole affair and demanded a refund, using him as a scapegoat for the whole disaster, as if it was the shoes that caused the grieving son to get drunk and drop the coffin.

But the woman who is approaching a style more reflective of her age never comes back to his establishment. He figures she's picked up her layers of accents off the shelf and gone back to that land far away from Jamaica where she lives.

*

Philip settles down in the armchair in the backroom of the parlour to have his lunch. He reaches over to a table close by and pours himself a cup of lukewarm tea. Then, a sound. Philip stops fixing his tea. There are footsteps in the front of the parlour: odd, because the chimes by the door have not announced anyone's arrival; and then, not so odd to Philip by now.

He continues to pour his tea and then stirs it.

The footsteps don't plod. They are quick and hesitant to the floor, like how a man walks in shoes a half size too small. Philip smiles, pleased with his generosity. It's common decency, he thinks to himself. Every man deserves shoes.

The quick hesitant steps of English loafers a half size too small enter his parlour, and blend well with the clip-clops of boots, and the squeesh-squeaks of slippers, and the tap-taps of church shoes. The sounds are not the kind which death can linger on; they are the sound of death itself.

Philip sips his tea, reflecting on many things at once. But foremost he reasons that there is always good company in his parlour, and he thinks again, with renewed conviction, and finally whispers it aloud, "Every man deserves shoes."

71

Sound Like a Gunshot
(three stories)

Salt

At 2 am, the shot was fired and Doris Gray's eyes opened wide. Her heart was racing, beating something like a kumina rhythm. She was confused, caught somewhere between the explosion and a dream she had been having, so she didn't even guess what had just happened.

The dream felt too real.

Michael was insisting, as usual, that she move out of the community. It seemed to Doris that since he had worked in a hospital for five years, and had earned himself thirty pounds of a solid beer gut, he felt he could boss everyone around. "It not safe here, Mama. This place is not what it used to be. The people you renting to are nothing but criminals. What happen when them get vex with you?"

"Tsssst. Chu man!" she dismissed him, "Look how long I live here! Nobody would dare trouble me."

"Then what about Sparky?"

How did Michael know about that? Doris wondered. Last week she had burst into Sparky's room and threatened him. Doris believed that you needed to be firm with tenants. "Listen Mister Sparky man! I don't care what kind of bad man you is, you not bad man for me. Pay me me money or else!"

The man was lying still on his bed, naked, puffing thick clouds of ganja into the air. He got up slowly and towered over Doris. "Or else what? Listen woman, is best you don't ramp with me."

When Monday morning came and he still had not paid,

Doris put all his things outside. The other tenants whispered that she was either brave or stark raving mad. Now in her dream, the fear that she had kept hidden, bloomed. "But Michael," she pleaded, "look how me old! As bad as Sparky be, him really wouldn't come do me nothin', eh?"

Michael didn't bother to answer. He started walking around the house, packing everything into a box he had under his arms. Doris was amazed to see how everything fit inside it: the furniture, her television, her clothes. Her whole life in one box!

"I think that's everything," he declared at last. She looked around to see the emptiness of the house she had lived in for thirty years. Michael hauled the box onto his head and balanced it. "Come now, Mama. We have to go."

Doris took his hand reluctantly and started walking. She whispered goodbye to each house that she passed, to the people that lived inside, to everything she knew about this place. Goodbye Leighton, Sandra, Maas Solomon, Chicken-eye and Daisy, Kitty. Goodbye Miss Samuel, Jerry B, Bulldog and Audrey. Goodbye Miss Lorinda.

She found it difficult to breathe. "Is a hard thing you making me do, you know Michael!"

"I know."

"I don't know how you did it! I don't know why you forcing me to do it now! You grew up with all these people."

"Is just a choice you have to make. Them have better places than this."

But Doris felt that she couldn't go any further. She had to go back. "Michael! That house is my whole life!"

"Which part of it is life, eeh? Which part? Every day another person dead, and you live there so long you start to think that is how people live. But people not supposed to go on like that. That is foolishness."

73

"I just can't, Michael."

"You have to."

"I said I can't!" and she looked back, tugged free from his hold, realizing too late that she made him lose balance of the box. She tried to reach out and catch it, but for some reason her arms were suddenly turning into salt, her legs too! Then her tongue dissolved into crystals; her eyes stung; her vision blurred. She only heard the great *boooodooooog!* when the box hit the ground – a sound like a gunshot – and she woke.

*

Caught between the explosion and the dream, Doris Gray could make no sense of what was actually happening. She didn't feel the red wetness pumping from out of her neck. She didn't see Sparky standing above her, gun pointed and smoking. She never heard when he said coldly, "You bitch, you! I tell you don't ramp with me."

Seer Woman

When Lorinda Matthews was six, her mother called her into the small kitchen with its moist amber light and discoloured linoleum floor and said, "Here, take this to your Granna. Be careful with it."

Lori sighed and took the glass of water. She hadn't yet learned the habit of whining about chores, but she always felt burdened to do anything for the sick, old woman they said was her Papa's mother.

See, Granna wasn't the kind of grandmother she heard her friends talk about: the kind who would sit in a rocking-chair and tell stories about the Old Days; the kind who would dance on occasion just to make the younger ones laugh; the kind who walked to market and back with groceries for the family. No. Granna was the kind of old woman who stayed in bed all day, trembling; who never remembered your name; who would pee-pee up herself and worse, so you had to clean her and bathe her throughout the day. Lori was scared of her Granna and hated to venture into that cold bedroom.

That morning, when Lori resentfully carried the glass of water, the first thing she realized was that the old woman was not shaking, that her eyes were open and she wasn't even blinking.

"Granna," Lori whispered, lightly tapping the woman's pale, wrinkled hand, "Granna. Granna. Granna!" The child growing angry because she didn't understand why this old woman wouldn't just sit up and drink the water so she could leave. "Granna! Granna! Granna!" And all of a sudden it dawned on the child. She had heard scary stories of this but had never seen it for herself. Her grandmother who she had always been a little scared of, was now a Dead Somebody! Lorinda dropped the glass of water and screamed.

The funeral was hard on the child. She didn't want to go. Lori had entered the church in the arms of her father, hugging him tight, looking behind on the rows and rows of people in black. It was when he stopped for a few seconds and bowed his head and she could feel him trembling with grief, that she twisted herself around and found herself looking down on the powdered, dead face of her grandmother.

Every night she began having this dream of Granna sitting down in the red living-room armchair with her toothless smile, and Lori would bolt straight out of her sleep. "Is awright," Mrs Matthews tried to comfort her daughter on these nights, "Is just because we don't send the spirit off yet. But we soon do that. Don't worry, child."

Finally the Ninth Night came. People crammed into the

small house to send the spirit of Granna off properly. Lori's parents tried to keep an eye on her even as they were saying hello and offering soup or bully-beef sandwich and juice to all the relatives and friends and acquaintances who piled in. They were happy when they saw her in the living room inquisitively touching one of the big bass drums brought in for the singing. They were even happier when she sat down beside the drum, when she yawned and fell asleep right there, on the floor. The past two weeks had been so stressful for the little girl, she needed the rest.

When they were ready to start the ceremony, Mrs Matthews had every intention of picking up Lori and putting her in her bed. In fact, she was on her way to do just that but was interrupted by someone asking her where exactly the bathroom was. She didn't see when the drummers took their seats; when the fool-fool bass drummer took up his instrument and smiled down at the child; when he nudged the other drummers, grinning mischievously, and placed the opening of the drum over the child's face. Mrs Matthews only turned around to see his hand high in the air, coming down fast. She wanted to shout out *No!* but it was too late. He hit out the sharpest bass sound she had ever heard, and Lori woke up screaming again.

The child looked around the room and kept on at a fever pitch. Her mother was also shouting in the background, "How you can wake up the child sudden like that! What is wrong with you?"

Lori was panicked, spinning all around the room, crying at full force because she didn't see her mother. In fact, she didn't see anyone she knew and there were lots and lots of people in the room. Pale figures, all of them, looking at her quietly. Most of them were old; a lot of them were dressed in fashions she had never seen before. Many of them had serious scars, or didn't have legs or ears, or their necks were broken. Just as suddenly as she had started screaming, she became quiet.

She could hear her mother now, "Look on that though eeh man! The child not even acting like she here. Lorinda baby?"

Lori still couldn't see her. She turned, looking around the whole room. She turned again, and again, and finally she looked to the red living-room armchair, and there was her Granna, sitting, smiling.

*

When the gunshot sounded that morning – a sound like a bass drum – Miss Lorinda kept her eyes closed and stayed in the bed for a while. She was a sixty-year-old woman and she knew all too well the danger of opening her eyes suddenly; there were always enough problems to handle without a thousand and one ghosts yap-yapping in her ears, telling her what they wanted, asking her the way to Jerusalem.

Finally she forced herself out of the bed. She needed to see if she was in any danger, and she wanted to find out which madman it was shouting out there like a real jackass since right after the shot – shouting something she couldn't make out. She walked to the window that was really just a space in the wall with a curtain covering it, pushed away the flimsy cloth and looked outside to the darkness.

The shouting stopped, but there in the middle of the street was her friend, Doris Gray. Doris looked around vacantly as if she hadn't come to grips with the fact that she was dead. Miss Lorinda sighed deeply. The ghost began moving up the road, up, up, out of the community. *Don't look back,* Lori thought. *Just keep on walking.*

Sparky

"You bitch you! I tell you don't ramp with me" he said, looking away as his mother held her stomach. Tasha could not believe the boy had really kicked her. She looked up at him wide-eyed, her mouth open as if it was never going to release the breath it held.

Sparky tried not to meet her stare because he wanted to feel justified in the knowledge that he had warned her, in his gut feeling that she was too weak and deserved it, but he saw her eyes and knew what she was thinking and it hurt him. She was thinking, *My God! You is just like you daddy!*

The man whom he thought of as his father was Mr Samuels, a married man who lived with his real family on some hill in St Andrew, Sparky was never sure which one. Mr Samuels didn't look anything like the boy, but he came to the yard regularly and sometimes even spent the night. He did two things which Sparky saw as paternal: he gave them, Sparky and his mother, money all the while and he beat the two of them regularly. So Sparky called him Daddy, and it seemed to amuse the man who might well have been the actual father. His mother wasn't sure.

When Sparky was fifteen, and growing used to his muscles, he slowly began to resent Mr Samuels and hate his mother for her weakness. He now saw his "Daddy" as a fat drunkard and vowed he wasn't going to take another beating from him. That was how the fight started – the one in which Sparky held the strap Mr Samuels was about to hit him with, kicked the man to the floor, fell on top of him and began pounding his face brutally with punches. Obese and intoxicated, Mr Samuels couldn't do anything but receive his bruises whimpering. He cursed Tasha for raising a violent ghetto child, cursed her and her son for being ungrateful bastards, and swore he was never coming again.

But he did come again, after only a month, ignoring the ghetto child and choosing now to beat only Tasha. Sparky covered his ears many nights, just not to hear her crying, or Mr Samuels slapping her, and his disgust for both of them grew.

When he was seventeen, Sparky felt more than ready to leave his mother's house, but she objected. "How you going to live, eeh? How you going to live! You think you is any man yet?"

He ignored her. He had gone over it too many times, that he could make money from hustling same as he was doing now, that he had found a place in Duck's Town where he and Jamie and Franko were going to live, that he was going to do this, no matter what.

"Sparky! Listen to me, man! Listen me. You can't leave."

She started crying, and the hatred he had nursed for her and her weakness rose to his throat. He spat. "Just leave me alone yaa."

"No! No!" and she started grabbing for his things, grabbing the bag he was putting his clothes in, taking things out and throwing them on the floor.

"Mama, stop ramping wid me! Stop ramping wid me t'ings."

"No. I not making you leave. You too hard ears. You staying right here, man! You going to stay," messing up his careful packing, throwing them here and there, ripping open the plastic bags he had stuffed some shirts in.

"Mama! Me say stop ramp with me! Jesus Christ!"

But she wouldn't stop, and that was why he kicked her, kicked her hard. She fell on the floor, held her stomach and fresh tears sprang up to her eyes. She looked at him like she was seeing him for the first time and her mouth opened wide at the shock of it all.

Sparky looked away. "You bitch you. I tell you don't ramp with me." He left her like that, and never saw her again.

*

Sparky fired the gun and he didn't know what made him repeat those words. Probably it was Doris's frozen stare and her mouth opened wide, sucking down a final breath that reminded him of his mother, and so he automatically said it.

But the sound of the gunshot was ringing in his ear. He couldn't hear anything. He couldn't hear himself, and all of a sudden he wondered if Doris understood that she had provoked this. He wondered if his mother understood that she deserved the kick he had given her, because she was ramping with him, and don't him did warn her? Don't? So he said again, "I did tell you, bitch. I did tell you! Why you don't listen, eh?" The sound of the shot was still in his ear, so he had to say it louder, then louder again and all he wanted was for Doris to understand, for his mother to understand. "I did tell you don't ramp with me! I did tell you!"

Doris's face was frozen in death, her wide-mouthed gaze making that constant accusation, *My God! You is just like you daddy!* Sparky felt a nausea climb into his stomach and rise up to his throat. He covered his mouth, ran outside into the yard and vomited. Then his knees buckled. He fell on the ground and wept.

Blood on the Door

The blood will be a sign for you on the houses where you are;
and when I see the blood I will pass over.
Exodus

Sister Inez, who keep in tune to the world by listening to her radio day in and day out, heard it first. She haul up her skirt by the hem, ran outside and shouted the news, "Flood water! Hurricane a come!"

Everyone panicked. It was going to happen again, just as it did in 1988. Whatever hinged the heavens up in space had loosened, and the sky was going to crash down. The winds would gather and the waters would rise.

Ten years ago the sky fell. They told us hurricane was nothing but a lot of rain, but when we lock up in the houses and we hear the animals we tie up outside crying out when them breathe in the water and them chests burst open, and we hear trees falling and the rain pounding and things hurling into the walls, we say that is not just rain... is the sky fall down baam! and destroy everything.

When the waters left and the sky rose back up to its usual place, we went outside. All the animals dead and some houses that we knew to be in one place, was in another place. Some houses we never saw again, and they find three bodies at the bottom of the gully, almost washed out to sea. It was destruction and death, wearing faces we had not seen before.

Now, the first man I see die, with my own two eyes I see it, was Old Man. Old Man so old that no one could remember his right age, or him having any other name. But old as him was, it never had to be his time. Him lock up in that house and couldn't get no food, and so sick and shame him couldn't come out to ask nobody for help and when we find out it was too late. Is me, little girl that I was at the time, who hold him small head in my lap, his eyes yellow and sink in, and I try to feed him. But him lips wouldn't open. That is how it come, destruction and death, bad luck so hard and so real, you could touch it and put it right there on your what-not beside the porcelain, and say, "See is why I can't move out of this shit house. See there is what tie me down!" But in 1988, destruction and death catch us by surprise, for we never knew they came in wind and in sky.

So when Sister Inez run outside like old time warner woman from out of the hills, come to tell us 'bout impending doom, we all looked up and crouched, 'cause now we knew how heavy the sky could hit you. We packed up fast to leave. Suitcases had our clothes and our lives. We put the little money we had in plastic bags, lodged it between our breasts. Everybody hand full, and we march out with the animals to higher ground where the radio said was safe.

But is not everyone pack up. A few stayed – those who really believe they could face the sky again. They was mostly men who did nothing but idle by the shop, playing dominoes and laughing at everybody who pass them, and I feel is just the liquor that was in them stomach and in them head that pin them down to that death trap. But on the march out, the rain already drizzling, there was baby mothers who flung themselves in the middle of the road bawling, and then they get up to cuss bad words so bad old women had to cork the children's ears. What else to do when a woman really upset but to cry and cuss bad words? And is through the crying and the cussing that they manage to drag some of the men from the rum shop.

But there was a woman who stayed back as well. Miss Yvonne. A plump dark lady with large breasts and grey streaks in her thick hair, who had raised six sons and buried one. She took the five boys – the oldest was sixteen and the youngest was seven – and her animals in the walls she believed would be salvation.

Miss Yvonne even stand up in her doorway the evening and offer her house as a shelter. "Come people! Come! Don't mind how the house small. We all can stay in here. Nothing going to touch this house." I thinking, she was just like Noah, calling the heathens to find refuge in her house; and we was just like the heathens, 'cause we laughed at her. The house was small in truth, and if we never dead from the hurricane, we would dead from suffocation. "Is awright, Miss Yvonne. We going where the man on the radio say is safe."

So the woman who had five sons left, locked her door tight and there was a feeling of safety inside. Even the oldest boy, who could hardly remember a hurricane when he was six, took comfort in the words his mother keep repeating like a psalm, "It will pass us over. Trust me," she whispered, "trust me."

Miss Yvonne believed this with all her heart because there was blood on her door.

*

Miss Yvonne boy William was never really bad. Yes he had a gold tooth and a long scar cross him left cheek, and him did walk with a swing and a dip in him shoulders, but is just so you have to move if you live where we live. But William not troubling nobody and him polite and generous to most people. A slight temper yes, I give you that. Still, everybody I know from George's Park have a slight temper. William was just ordinary... nobody that we did form any big opinion of, not until them spread him name cross newspaper. But sometimes papers have a mind of their own and say what they want to say. And sometimes there is a story behind a story. So I can tell you, William was not no area don.

But Miss Yvonne first-born get cut down early. Too early. Is the fair skin woman him used to do yard work for, put down eight thousand dollar on the lamp table by the door and when she come back she never see it. Same time she screw up her face and walk outside asking for the "Dutty yard bwoy" and when William come she say she want back the money now. Poor William, trying hard not to make him slight temper show and him answer politely, "Ma'am, I don't know what you talking about."

The lady stand up firm with her hands akimbo, and say, "Listen here! I can't bother with the thieving likes of you people. Just give me back the money and get out or I'm calling the police!"

William slight temper get out that time, and him raise the cutlass and in two twos him rest the blade against her neck. Her skin like it get grey that time and all the power drain from her body, for in an instant she became a little old woman begging for her life. But William not troubling nobody, you understand. Him only look on her and say, "Listen, I don't got no money for y-y-you..." And him stammer on the rest and just never say any more. Is the speech him wanted to give. The same speech that all of us with no opportunity have well up in we belly and we want to tell it to the powers that be one day. But we don't know how to say it ourselves, so we listen to Garvey, and Martin Luther King, and when Bob Marley say, "We belly full but we hungry", we spirits nod for him find the words that we can't say ourselves. William let the cutlass fall from him hands and him walk off, both him and the lady crying. She thanking God to save her life from this vicious black man. Him cry because him belly full, but him hungry still.

William walk all the way home, and we knew not to say anything to him, for him walk straight without any swing or dip and a man round here only walk like that when him vex for true. And somehow when we saw the police Land Rover ease into the district like some western movie, like some sheriff and him posse riding silent into town, when we see that, we know. We know them was coming to William for is so trouble always happen around here. They drive straight behind the man they see walking with a slight temper. Four of them in the vehicle, with guns pointing outside the window, into the sky. The driver ask, "Is you name William?"

But is like William never hear for him reach him gate and turn in and walking towards the door of that grey wooden house. The police car stop and them pile out and them ask again, angry this time, "Hey bwoy! We ask if is you name William."

William turn round to them, and so much hate was in him eyes, the police decide for true is him that did rob and attempt murder on the white woman on the hill. And I don't know exactly what William say but I feel is probably the speech him trying to get out of him belly again, for there are times when the speech is like it rise to our throats and we almost choke on it. But whatever him say or half say, it get the police angry, for in a moment gun was drawn and shot was fired and William dropping and him gushing blood. Blood. Blood. And him dead with the hate still in him eyes. Him dead. Dead. Miss Yvonne run out and hold him limp head in her lap and pray hard, so hard. She praying to God but she remembering a turtle. And later she tell us though she prayed, she knew it was in vain, for she heard about the time when the world was still young and two turtles try to take the moon and a dead man cross a river; the one with the moon sink a little but then come up safely on the other side but the one with the corpse sink and drown with the weight. And from then on a dying moon returns, but not a dead man.

A white lady on a hill wake up the next morning to find eight thousand dollars had fallen behind the table and ever since she twitched nervously with guilt. But that wasn't the story in the newspaper. They reported instead on an area don who opened fire on police, and the police returned fire and killed him.

We scrambled in front of the news camera to set the record straight and to say he was a good boy. Him not troubling nobody. But Martha who do domestic work up in the hills say she see us on TV and her heart swell with pride and sadness, but her boss kiss him teeth and switch the channel and say, "Is so them damn fools always protect those criminals!"

When the news people left, we went to Miss Yvonne, for there were things to do there. Men cooked curry goat and played drums and set out the white rum. Older women sang soft and low like sorrow itself, causing a lump in throats, "Bawl woman bawl / If yu nuh bawl, if yu nuh cry / if water nuh come a yu eye / Yu body and yu soul will part / Bawl woman bawl and ease yu heart", and they sang "Holy, holy, holy Mount Zion", and they sang "Roll, Jordan, roll!"

I came with wash brush and soap powder and bleach, and we start from the walk way removing the blood stains, and working our way up to the door. But when we reach there Miss Yvonne come out, her eyes red from easing her heart and rolling Jordan, her breasts not looking as robust as their usual self and she looking frail in spite of her plumpness. "No. Don't touch the door," she say to us, "for I can't take no more grief. Leave the blood of me first-born there, so the Lord will have mercy and pass me over."

William's blood stayed on the door, and is like it did protect the family for true. For when the water in the tank was contaminated and everybody get sick and three children died, Miss Yvonne and her house drink the pipe water same way and not a thing happen to any of them. The year when they complain that we living on "capture land" and they threaten to remove the squatters, them come and demolish the house on Miss Yvonne's left and on her right. But nobody touch her house, and before they could return we block road and push up we face in news camera again and cry for injustice and them stop bother us 'bout we squatting. Is not one or two times gun war break out in George's Park and every house have bullet holes in the zinc to prove it. But not a bullet even graze Miss Yvonne house after William dead and she said there was power in the firstborn's blood to save her from destruction and death. And that is why when she heard the sky was going to fall, Miss Yvonne stayed right where she was.

*

The hurricane came at the hour the sun should have risen. So it was like night just carried on forever. The rain start to fall and the boys laugh to each other and ask "Is this the people them a go on so bad over?" They agreed that it was good to have excuse not to go to school, but why Courtney and Portia from next door, and all the neighbours in fact, had to leave on account of simple rain was beyond them. So it never take too long for them to open the door which Miss Yvonne had locked tight, and go outside – just because sometimes it sweet to play in the rain, and in all fairness they was only children, and children is always careless and stupid. The two older ones just stand up under the awning, getting wet but enjoying the rain and, in a quiet way, grudging the smaller boys who could go all out and play in the mud and the rivers which formed, and in the puddles. They ask each other again, "Is really this the people them a go on so bad over?" and they sucked their teeth. But then the sky blaze up and lightning strike the big mango tree and one of the biggest branches crash down right in front of two of the boys, and when the muddy water splash them good and proper, it never seem like too much fun again. Without looking at each other, without even saying a word, they all agree it was time to go back inside.

They lock the door behind them and dry off quick before Miss Yvonne could see their wetness and give them a sound beating. The rain had gotten heavier and their questions were different. For now it seemed in truth, that Portia and Courtney and all the neighbours did really have sense. "Mama, you sure we awright?" The sky outside blazed up and a thunder like Armageddon shook the old house, and they couldn't hear when their mother answered, "It will pass."

Miss Yvonne look like confidence itself. The wind not shaking her faith, and the darkness outside not scaring her. She sat and sang, "There is power, power, wonder working power in the blood." She sat there so still and calm because she believed; but also it was because her mind was far away on other things.

She was remembering her first boy William, who for true was never really bad, and get cut down so early. The first child who she ever put to her breast, and who needed her, and made her feel like a woman, not no "wut'less girl who gone a road go breed" like her father had said, but a woman just like her mother and her grandmother, and the countless millions, billions who bore labour pains to bring people into the world. She found a humble job, sweeping hair from the floor of a barber's shop and it was never ever shameful work. Never. She was looking after another life, earning money to feed him and clothe him and give him opportunity. In him she find it was better to give than to receive, and she loved him. She loved him so much a tear rolling down her face now. For she wondering why the damn turtle had to drown – but then there was Lazarus and even when him dead dead dead and the worms start to take over his body, even then Jesus call him back, so why him couldn't call back her son!? And Lord, she thinking now, that is not just for protection sake make her keep the blood on the door, but is 'cause is William life. Not like the memories she have of him, not like the pictures or him baby clothes that she keep at the bottom of a box underneath her bed. Not like anything him did have with him in life. No. The blood was his actual life. It was a thing that was inside him, and kept him smiling and walking with a swing and a dip. The same blood which flood him head one day when a man tell him to go suck him modder, and William never back down, him pick a fight though this man had a weapon; and it was the same blood which drip down him face when the man give him a long scar across his cheek, blood he had shed for her.

Outside, the waters were rising and washing away the earth. More trees had fallen 'cause they couldn't stand up against the lightning or the hard rain digging away the dirt from beneath them. The wind and the rain moved together, plotted together and destroyed together. And suddenly they noticed this little grey wooden house standing up in the middle of all their work like it was laughing at them. So the wind and the rain decide they would try their hardest to swallow it. They turned. They pelted the walls and the door like they wanted to dissolve it, to tear it down. The door stood up strong though; the rain only succeeding in cleaning the mud and the grime from it. The mud and the grime and the blood. The water tore into the stain and slowly lifted it, till red water ran down and all that began to show was wood.

The children inside all scream out loud, for is the same time all of them feel something cold and slimy bite their heels, and they look down to see that the water was coming in. They look outside in terror but could see little, for everything was black. It was as if the sky and everything was one, like they was in a dark heaven already.

Their mother walked around confidently, as if she was walking on dry land. She sang loud now with the drumming the rain did on the roof, "There is power, power, wonder working power in the blooood of the laamb!" For in her heart of hearts she believed there was still blood on the door. Even as the water rose to her knees, she had no fear. But the children all now crying, and thinking of bad luck. Bad luck so hard and so real you can touch it and put it on the what-not beside the porcelain, and say, "See! See there is what tie me down!"

The Fear of Stones

And we think of our children and the stones upon their future
and we want these stones to move.
Lorna Goodison

1.

Here is what I believe: in this world, we are each an equation. For every moment a man lives, he is delivered once again through the short parallel lines of an equal sign. This is the story of Gavin. As such, it can be summed up: *stonebirth + harbour + chickenpox-at-5 + St Richard's Primary + Vineyard Town + Darren + Sylvia + the rain + the house behind the cane + cartoons on JBC + Vocational Bible School at Bethlehem Church of Christ + the smell of mosquito destroyer + every goddamned thing that happened in every goddamned moment of his life and then before =* Gavin.

That would be the short version. The long version, of course, is his actual life. This is only a telling, and every story is abridged. Who can waste time accounting for each insignificant breath taken? And who would even remember it all? But that fact is also part of this story – because if the rule really does exist that we each lose large portions of our lives to a kind of amnesia, then Gavin is the exception. His memory is its own universe, always expanding, stretching, inventing new spaces. If you give him enough time, Gavin would remember everything. He would remember his life from the beginning.

He would remember the evening on the Palisadoes Strip.

*

The man and woman were so in love, she had listened spellbound while he described to her the boring details of how the Strip was formed. It was evening, the sky was purple, which made the waters on either side look dark and thick like paint. Small crabs were running between the rocks. He parked his white Ford Escort on the sand and explained to her how Hope River emptied on to the sea, not far from where they were, and all the sand particles it brought out built up over thousands of years, and formed this five mile strip – Kingston Harbour on the inside, the Caribbean Sea on the out.

Gavin would remember how, a little later, the woman was sitting on the bonnet, her hand lifted in a kind of salute to shield her eyes from the setting sun. She was looking up on an Air Jamaica plane coming in for landing. It was so low she could read the writing on its belly. The man's back was to her by this time, his long hair gathered in a ponytail. He had been skipping stones across the water, but paused also to watch the landing. They were looking up awed, as if the contraption of metal above them was itself a part of the surrounding nature, had blossomed into being, along with harbour and sand and palm trees, when God said the word that unfolded creation.

They were not religious people. So it was strange, the shared gaze, the "beholding". Their eyes filled with all the certainty of faith, like wise men bewitched by a star. But they were in love. So you might as well forgive them their bedazzled eyes, the way they each thought stupidly upon seeing the aircraft, *Oh look! A plane! It must be a sign!*

Now, even a limousine is a better metaphor for the luxury of love; the stretching nature of it, the way "hi" becomes "hiiiiiii", as if the speaker is willing time to slow down. But a plane? It doesn't make sense. Yet this is the colonizing way of love, this ability to own everything, to see and transform things in impossible ways. Love will see a pile of cowshit in the middle of Hope Gardens, and say, "How absolutely beautiful!" – not because it has X-ray vision and sees a daisy seed hidden in its centre that will burst out in all radiance in another month, but rather because love is silly, and also – the cliché – it is blind.

When the plane dipped below a copse of trees, bringing the couple's gazing to an end, they exhaled together. The man, Darren, bent to pick up another stone and Sylvia, the woman, returned to watching him – his back, slender and elegant in the white merino he had on. He had taken off his long-sleeved shirt soon after they arrived, gave it to her with a kind of chivalry that didn't suit the landscape, that probably came from watching too many movies. He said to her, "Here, it can get windy." And though the breeze turned out to be a warm one, the kind you opened yourself to, still she held his shirt tightly around her shoulders. Watching him – his back, his hand extended, poised to throw – she suddenly saw the green and purple glint of the stone under the last of the sun's light and shouted, "No!"

Sylvia jumped off the car, ran over to him.

"Look on it," she lifted his own hand to his face, showing him the stone his fingers were still curled around. "You can't throw this away, Darren. Look how it so beautiful."

He turned it around and agreed, "It pretty for true," and slipped it into his pocket. "But now look how you get sand all over my shirt, eeh?"

She looked behind and laughed at the sight of the shirt, crumpled on the ground.

*

If you give him enough time, Gavin could remember all of that. He doesn't right now and for a very good reason – he has no business remembering it; he wasn't there. It took place in 1977, the year before he was born, before he was even conceived; the year in which, if he was anything at all, it was only a vague idea never even spoken between Darren or Sylvia.

So how is it that Gavin remembers everything that happened the next day?

October 1st, 1977. On the stroke of midnight it started to rain. The exact moment when it stopped being September, officially turned into "the wet month", the clouds on cue began to empty themselves, as if they had been waiting, had received their orders and had been counting down, three... two... one... thunder, lightning, rain! However, it was the kind of downpour that slips into the background, becomes white noise. You are lulled into deep sleep. Night extends way into morning. Birds are kept away. The sun is behind the clouds. So at 11 am that morning, Sylvia was still in her bed.

Windshield wipers working frantically, Darren's Ford Escort made its way slowly up the puddle-filled avenue of Vineyard Town. He parked, opened his door and emerged, umbrella first. He had not realized that as soon as the car had stopped, so had the rain. Ironic really, that the one time when the world actually did stop to acknowledge their love, to give Darren and Sylvia a symbol, a sanction, neither of them recognized it.

But it didn't go completely unnoticed. Sylvia's mother, Miss Betty, who had been sitting on the patio, saw when the car drove up, saw when the rain stopped, saw Darren step out of the car, and thought to herself with some amount of resignation, *So this is how it is, eh!*

Darren walked up the steps and the old woman stood up to meet him. "Sylvia still sleeping."

He looked disappointed. Miss Betty's face softened. "Come inside, nuh," she said, "while Sylvia get herself ready."

"Th-thank you," Darren stammered. It was the first time Miss Betty had invited him in. He sat in the dimly lit room while Sylvia got ready, amazed how the inside of every

Jamaican house could look so similar: always a portrait of Jesus hanging, hair perfectly permed, his hands clasped, his blue eyes looking to heaven; always the same over-polished shelf crowded with cheap porcelain animals, the same vase of plastic flowers in the centre; the same embroidered "God Bless Our Home" on the wall; and the same beaded curtains to separate the living room from the kitchen. But it was the sofa and chairs that got to Darren. No doubt purchased five, maybe ten years ago. A sensible purchase at the time. A sign of domesticity and of moving upwards. A sofa and matching chairs with cushions, bought from a store! Yet, in the scheme of things, no one could have been really confused, could they? It *was* bought from a store, but it had likely been the cheapest set, the one all the truly advanced people walked past, the one that was put on sale just to get rid of it. In its boring design, its rigid angles, its uncomfortable rectangularity, the sofa set was as much a sign of poverty as it was of advancement. And so it really did get to Darren, how after five, maybe ten years, the chairs were still in their original plastic cover. The thick yellow of age was now spreading itself across. He wondered, sitting there, about the things old people will hold on to: gas lighting, red floors that could never be polished, and now, plastic separating you from the softness underneath. And maybe, Darren thought, it was not a holding on, but an inability to let go of hardness. That perverse love Caribbean people will never admit to, of sunhot and whips.

"Darren?"

He looked up and smiled. It was Sylvia. She had finally stepped out, smelling of carbolic soap and mint. Everything about her was unpretentious and beautiful: her low afro, the small silver studs in her ears, the dashiki dress stopping right before her knees, her long legs, the leather sandals, the absence of nail polish, lipstick or eyeshadow. There were times he felt fake beside her, wondered why she dated someone like him. He who had greased his hair so much that very day that its straightness was exaggerated, its sheen blinding. His hair, so terrific in its Indian-ness that sometimes you doubted he was mixed with anything else. She never questioned this obsession with hair, only laughed when he, out of lifetime habit, hit her hand away whenever she tried to touch it.

There will actually come a day – to be specific, a year and two months from now, in 426 days – such will be Darren's grief that he will shave his head bald. With one hand, he will hold the baby he has named Gavin to his chest, and with the other he will throw the shaven hair on top of the coffin that is being lowered into the earth. Then, he will turn away, sobbing, and will not realize that in this motion he has dropped the two-week-old baby. He will not miss the weight and he will not hear the child hollering; he will simply walk away. But all of this is to come... in time, in time. Let us concentrate on October 1st, 1977. Sylvia in her dashiki dress, Darren smiling. He asked, "So you ready?" She said yes; turned to her mother, "I'll be back before dark, Mums."

They walked in single file towards the door, Darren in front, Miss Betty at the back as if ushering them out. Then suddenly, before stepping outside, Darren remembered something. He stopped, turned to Sylvia, reached into his pocket and took out a necklace. It was really a stone pendant hung on a leather string, the stone varnished, wrapped around with wire. She looked at it and saw that it was the stone she had saved the day before.

"Darren Williams! O God, you made this for me?"

He hung it around her neck and she beamed, the comfortable weight of stone resting between her breasts, and Miss Betty thought for the second time that day, *So this is how it is, eh?*

They went to Hope Gardens, spread a blanket under the arch of an aqueduct – an aqueduct that was used to water plantations (and excuse the intrusion, but what is so romantic about these vestiges of slavery? Carriage rides; a couple, hand in hand looking over the sprawl of a cane field; getting married in the shadow of Rose Hall Great House; a picnic under the arch of an aqueduct? But perhaps I'm not qualified to theorize on history. My PhD is in Mathematics. I did a dissertation on Complex Analyses. And I do not mean to taint this day for Darren or Sylvia. Because it was a beautiful day). They sat on that blanket, the grass beneath it still wet, ate sandwiches, drank apple juice. A vendor passed them, trying to sell peppered shrimps. Darren said, "I will buy a bag if you take a picture of us," and handed the man his camera.

Frozen forever, this window onto October 1st, 1977. Darren, his luxurious hair stiff in the afternoon breeze, Sylvia in her brown dashiki dress, a stone glinting purple and green between her breasts. Them holding hands on a blanket spread under an arch, smiling an honest smile. Comfortable. In love. This is the picture...

... the picture Gavin's grandmother, Miss Betty, gave him when he was seven and he asked her how his momma looked. She gave him a shoebox, and in it was the necklace – varnish stripping, the leather warm and mouldy. And under the stone pendant, this picture that Gavin cried over after his grandmother left the room. He took it with him to school, to church, to the bath. The picture that after a year was crushed and stained beyond recognition, but by which time the image was imprinted on his mind.

*

If children really are the great imaginers, is it possible that this is the seed of Gavin's memory? That studying that picture day in and day out, he himself invented a whole story around it, an elaborate story with rain and aqueducts and peppered shrimp?

It is possible.

2.

Consider now a fairy tale – *Beauty and the Beast, Cinderella* or *Sleeping Beauty*. Let us go to the bone of the story, the part they never tell us, the implicit suggestion: boy meets girl; girl is attractive, boy is (or will become) handsome enough but, more importantly, he is stable; they are both virgins, the girl in particular has never seen an erect penis; on their wedding night they have sex and on that same night the girl becomes pregnant.

On February 14th 1978, Valentine's Day, Sylvia and Darren were married; girl, gorgeous as ever; boy set to inherit his father's haberdashery store – in other words, stable. That evening, they went into their hotel room, tentative and excited as they peeled off each layer of clothes – the veil, the gloves, the heels; the bow-tie, the jacket, the vest. Later on she bled a little as if this was her gift to him and he reciprocated by filling up her womb.

The fairytale continues – well what else would you call it – that at the very moment Sylvia conceived, she knew! The knowledge was not a comfortable one. It announced itself as a grain of sand swimming somewhere in her centre. Tiny. Darren fell asleep, as men will do, exhausted and thrilled with the loss of his virginity. She turned to her left, to her right, to her left again, trying to get rid of this foreign thing inside her, to shift it, to allow her body to swallow it. Eventually she sat up, swung her feet off the bed, focused on this grain of sand, tried gently to cough it up.

Sylvia smiled for the rest of their honeymoon, determined not to ruin it. She even smiled for her first four weeks back at work, teaching Grade Five students, the other teachers flocking around her, winking, pinching her, asking "How was it?" She smiled for them. She smiled for her husband. But after five weeks the grain of sand had not gone anywhere. It had grown into a stone, a very small stone like a piece of gravel. Now she was lying awake at nights, coughing louder, harder, until finally she would sit still considering this new thing inside her, trying to guess its shape.

The discomfort became painful. So she went to Darren and told him the truth, her voice trembling, "Is like I feel a stone lodged inside me." She touched her navel. "I can't describe it any better than that. I just don't feel good."

"What you really saying?" there was concern in his voice but he didn't understand.

She was crestfallen. She had secretly hoped he would have had the answer.

He touched her gently and she started to weep.

The next day they headed out for the doctor. The nurse, an old woman who didn't seem to know how to smile, told Darren to wait outside. He read all kinds of women's magazines, checked his watch every thirty seconds, looked up and followed the cracks which ran like spider veins across the ceiling. Finally, the door opened. The doctor himself stepped out, smiling broadly. Darren allowed himself to hope. Nothing could be wrong... could it? The doctor was smiling. He walked over, sat down, patted Darren on his knee and delivered the news, "There's nothing I can see that's wrong with your wife. And I suspect she is in the very early stages of pregnancy."

Darren's peal of laughter cut across the office like an explosion, at which the unsmiling nurse stumbled backwards behind her desk and almost fell.

"Pregnant! Pregnant! We going to have... Pregnant!" Darren ran into the doctor's office where Sylvia was still sitting. He grabbed her by the waist and lifted her in the air. "Sylvia. You see! Everything going to be okay! You going to have a baby."

She looked down on him and tried to smile. Failed. She had been smiling for over a month. Her face sagged. He put her down slowly. "Baby, what wrong now? Don't you see is nothing to be worried about? We going to have a child!"

She wanted to explain it to him, that she knew all this already. She didn't come here to find out she was pregnant. She wanted to know why the pregnancy felt so wrong.

*

Here is a bit of flawed logic: for everything that exists, there is a word. If there is not a word for something, then it stands to reason, the thing does not exist. For example, what is the opposite of erosion? How does a stone grow? There is no word for such a process, it does not exist. How does a stone grow? It does not. It cannot. Maybe then, we can understand Sylvia's response to her pregnancy: *This can't be happening!*

But Sylvia's pregnancy did happen. She carried the baby full term. So I will tell you how a stone grows: by geometric progression, a binary sequence – first it splits in two, then the two pieces split in four, four pieces in eight, then sixteen, thirty two, and so on and so on. In this sudden congregation of cells, there will soon be a spine, arms and legs, a face, eyes.

Three months into her pregnancy, Sylvia got up too quickly and fell. She had come home early from work that day, taken the bus home and despite feeling a little sick, decided she'd make dinner for herself and Darren. She put the white rice on to boil, with a spoon of butter on top. She cut up onions and green pepper, seasoned a few chicken parts while she let the curry burn slightly in the oil. She was an excellent cook when she was in the mood, and today she was in that mood. Sylvia then unpacked some of the gift boxes they still hadn't opened from the wedding, took out what she decided she would henceforth label as her "good plates", white and broad with a silver crest in the middle. She took out wine glasses because she decided even though there was no wine, tonight she and Darren would drink lemonade from long stemmed glasses, their pinkie fingers pointed out to mock how real uptown people did it. Sylvia laughed to herself at that image. When she was finished all the cooking and done dressing the table, she sat down to wait on Darren; and it was only a few more minutes before he turned the Escort into the driveway of their flat.

Darren opened the door to the hot smell of curry and boiled corn and white rice. "I see somebody loves me," he smiled at her.

"And you never realize that before I married you?" she laughed. "You better hope is not poison I set to poison you now."

He walked over to where she was sitting by the table, kissed her on the forehead. "Let me just take off these clothes." He went into the bedroom.

She got up to take the lemonade out of the fridge, but she got up too quickly. It was the weight inside her womb that unbalanced her – the thing that now felt as if a fist was tightly clenched inside her stomach, felt like she had swallowed a rock whole, one of those smooth stones you haul up from the bottom of a river, varnish and leave on your desk as a paperweight. She tried, as any falling person will, to hold on to something but only managed to grab the tablecloth. Dishes crashed on top of her and Darren ran out to find her slumped on the floor, not even crying or saying anything, stained with hot curry. "Sylvia? Sylvia?" He lifted her up, cooing to her softly, "Sylvia?", took her to the bedroom, laid her on the bed and wiped her face. "Sylvia, you okay?"

She still didn't answer him. Avoided his eyes.

"Sylvia? Sylvia, what you need me to do? You want us to go back to the doctor?"

She finally looked on him. Wanted to say, *Take me to one of them clinics so I can get rid of this. Please. Let me have an abortion. We will try this a next time...*

"Sylvia, anything. Just tell me."

She considered it but then shook her head and closed her eyes tightly. "Is okay, Darren. I just need to rest."

*

The dignity of the Caribbean woman is quite something. How she is, at heart, a chaos theorist – in her very genes it would seem, accepting the Law of Entropy. She expects tomorrow will be harder than today; that the money which bought meat this week will not be able to buy water next week; that things worsen; life is a constant worsening. And how she accepts the defeat of it all, and trudges on – that is something. Not beautiful, because suffering is never beautiful. But perhaps blessed. A lost beatitude: *Blessed are you when you suffer long, for surely you will see God soon.*

In the months while her body was being crushed (how else would you describe her pregnancy?), Sylvia learned that pain increases little by little, that a rock can spread itself out and that your insides can be ripped apart slowly. How did she handle it all? With dignity and gritted teeth.

But there is a point at which the strongest woman breaks, will lift up her skirt in front of the news cameras to show the world her cellulite rippled thighs and the pink flowers of her oversized panties; a reporter will be pointing a mike at her, and she will scream into it, *"Laaawdavemercy!"* Just that, because what else is there to say? "Laaawdavemercy!" Sylvia's breaking was literal, a sudden contraction that broke the amniotic sac of her womb, causing water to run down against her thighs and a sharp pain to rack her entire body. She opened her mouth and screamed a scream that had been nine months in the making, a terrible scream that came, unfortunately, just after Darren had crept out to go and buy another ream of white paper.

Is there any greater shame than this, that in her most critical moments, her husband was sneaking into his white Ford Escort, driving happily towards the pharmacy completely oblivious to the onset of his wife's labour. Shameful, that all he could think about, while she was at home bawling the life out of her lungs, was the cleanness of white paper, the potential a single sheet holds, how he would labour over it in the evening; because unbeknownst to Sylvia, Darren had discovered poetry.

A woman who is pregnant is slowly being separated from the world. She grows her own country, her own planet, and everyone else is on the outside. Everyone, even the father. He might put his ear against his wife's tummy, might sing, might read stories; it doesn't matter, he is on the outside. Add to this the fact of Sylvia's silent suffering, then imagine what it would do to a husband, to see his wife in pain and to be unable to do anything about it.

So Darren took to staying outside in the living room late at night, the bedroom being too depressing a place. He delayed going to sleep. He would sit around the table, read the books he now enjoyed, look at the walls, study his fingers. Then one night he scribbled on the empty back page of a James Baldwin novel, his first poem. The next night he wrote another poem, and the night after that another. Poems for his son and his wife, as if these were his maps, a way of finding his way back to them. But consider a fairytale: *Hansel and Gretel*, two stupid children wandering off into the woods, sprinkling crumbs behind them. They are not afraid, their confidence lying in a trail of crumbs which even then, they could not know, was being eyed by hungry birds. So isn't it ironic that the thing meant to lead them home ends up being the thing that takes them further and further away?

*

How does a woman give birth to a stone? Alone. In sweat and in tribulation. With weeping and the gnashing of teeth. Alone. The vagina must tear at the seams, the body must bleed. Heaving, the sheets drenched in blood and sweat. Screaming. Screaming. In pain. Her own body falling apart. Her nails sunk deep into the mattress, her head flung back, trembling. Crying. Pushing. Choking on the word "Laaawwdavemercy!" Pushing. In pain. In pain, and alone.

And now the stone is at the door – just one last push, one final push. Sylvia summons up her strength, focuses, pushes out the child in one great heave and shouts – for the nine months of discomfort, for the pain, for the hundred days of living on her back, for the stone she never loved – she shouts, *"OhLawdHaveMercyFuckYou…!"*

In a few minutes Darren will return and find the baby, beautiful, breathing on his own, lying between the legs of his mother's corpse, his eyes already open, not even crying. Imagine that, Darren will never know the first words spoken over the little boy's life were a curse – a curse delivered by a dying woman – *ohlawdhavemercyfuckyou!* What a way to enter the world.

The night done; the eye dumb; the stone born. The night done, the eye dumb, the stone is born.

3.

I can remember the first time my father beat me.

But that isn't the memory I wanted to share. I wanted to say that I remember being in Pennsylvania for the first time one summer, wide-eyed with the wonder of this thing they called America. I was driving in the back seat of my uncle's car. I remember him shooting through a red light and a man from the other side of the road also broke his red light, and because they were turning in the same direction, my uncle and this man end up smack in front of each other, and all I could reflect on, as my life was ready to close, were high school physics formulas: force = Mass x acceleration. Impact = Mass1 x Velocity1 added to Mass2 x Velocity2. These are, of course, stupid thoughts to die on. Both men had to slam on their brakes and the cars came to a skidding stop. The man in the other car stuck his head out the window in righteous indignation as if he hadn't just broken the law himself, and my uncle did the same. But there was something, something a little too mirrored, in the way they each knit their brows, or maybe it was the way they flung out their hands, or maybe it was the shape of their angry mouths, both wrapped around the exact same word, *Bumboclawt!* Whatever it was they recognized it in each other and, instead of cursing, they smiled. One said, "Yes Yardie! Respeck!" and the other, "Yah man. No problem."

Imagine that! What had originally seemed to be another way this bitch of a country was going to push them down, turned out to be divine appointment, the meeting of a fellow tribesman, turned out to be a message from God, *Behold, you are not alone!*

What I take from that scene is this amazing green and gold pride. This thing of being Jamaican.

I remember the first time my father beat me. I remember the green and gold pride. And I remember the beating and I remember the pride. And they become mixed up. It becomes mixed up for almost every Jamaican. We remember the parents that beat us, the aunts and uncles that beat us, the grandparents that beat us, the teachers that beat us. We remember shoes flung after us, belts and electric cords and stalks of bamboo breaking over our backs, and we are proud. We say, "That is what make us who we is!" But what is that? A nation of abused people? A country with repressed anger?

We watch the television. It is Christmas, and foreign children are opening their presents. A little girl gets a Barbie doll and her brother gets a truck. We laugh at this and say, "We never ever get no Barbie doll. We never get no truck. But we get some serious lick under we skin. And that was good."

Gavin does not need time to remember the way his grand-mother would beat him because time freezes around these incidents and we take them with us like photographs. He can retrieve it in an instant, the image of Miss Betty, belt doubled in her hand, shouting at him, "Take off you pants! Take it off." Nakedness, it seemed, was necessary for punishment, a way to shame the boy. After he dropped his pants, she would whip him over his entire body, on his thighs, his hands, his face, his toes. He danced this panicky dance, a desperate attempt to position his hands over the places he anticipated she was about to hit. He always anticipated wrong, so the bitter old woman, out of wind and panting, would continue to beat and beat him regardless, determined to use up her last breath punishing him for some crime or the other.

Backtrack: Gavin at nine years old was still beautiful. In fact it had become obvious his beauty was the kind that was never outgrown, a wonderful and lucky combination of genes. A handsomeness that was not tenuous, that did not have to rely on the absolute squareness and whiteness of his teeth (though they were square and very white and his smile was charming); that did not rely on his rigid cheekbones (though they were rigid and made his childish face look pretty); that did not rely on the loose curls of his dark brown hair, a shade which matched his skin exactly, or his large eyes, or anything else, because though his beauty included all of these, it did not depend on any one of them. And it was still there despite his heaviness, for Gavin was a round child. Round and insecure and completely unaware of his beauty.

Miss Betty was a supervisor at a restaurant that served lunch to several of the office workers in a busy section of downtown Kingston, a job she disliked and resented because it had never been her ambition. When she came home she was always tired, would plop herself down on the plastic-covered sofa and call, "Gavin! Gavin! Is which part you deh?"

Gavin was always in his room by the time she arrived, sometimes in his closet, sometimes under the bed trying hard to disappear, to become unnoticeable.

"Gavin!"

He would finally run out, "Yes Grandma?"

One time, the old woman gave the usual command, "Come me love. Me tired. Go in de kitchen and make me a cup of mint tea."

"Yes Grandma." And he ran outside to break off two stalks of mint. Went in and put on the kettle. Poured the hot water over the leaves. Made it sit. Took out the leaves, added sugar and a few teaspoons of condensed milk, stirred it, took it back out to her and waited in the shadows for her judgement.

Now a strange progression of thoughts happened in Miss Betty's mind after she took that first sip. First she thought, *Boy! This kinda sweet!* And then, *But this not good for my diabetes. But is like is kill this little pickney want to kill me, eh? Kill me. Just like*

how he kill his mother. Just like how he kill my little girl Sylvia.
Sylvia. Sylvia! Sylvia! She opened her mouth and shouted
"Laaawdavemercy!" and Gavin's heart grew cold, because he
knew he was in trouble.

"Gavin! Don't I show you by now how to make tea? Is what
happen, you dash way the whola de sugar in this?"

"N-n-no Grandma," almost ready to cry right then.

"Go and get me the belt. Go and get me the belt!"

He got it, gave it to her.

"Take off you pants! Take it off!" and then she beat him, the
same way she did almost every night. Because if it wasn't tea,
it was some homework he hadn't finished, some dish that had
broken, some out-a-order-ness she had spotted in his
demeanour that needed to be corrected, needed to be broken
out of him. There was always something, a reason to throw
back her head and say "Laaawdavemercy!" and then "Take off
you pants!" then lace the boy's behind until he was crying
hysterically, until he ran to his room to hug his pillow, to
tremble, to rock himself and try once more to disappear.

But a child who has just been beaten does not want to hug
a pillow. He does not want to fall asleep in the cold flesh of a
mattress.

Miss Betty, tired and spent all over again, would be sitting
in the sofa, her hand with the belt limp at the side, her huge
stomach rising and falling. Then after many minutes, Gavin
would creep up to the doorway, sucking his thumb, and peep
out at her. She knew he was there, but she always waited a
long while before looking up and into his beautiful eyes. Then
and only then would a feeling of guilt lodge into her throat;
only then might she think, *But after all! He lose Sylvia too, and*
worse he have no father to look up to. Sometimes she would say
to herself, *But you know he really not all that bad. For I teach him*
to be mannersable and in truth, he really does have manners more

*than most. And I teach him to pick up after himself and he do it.
And I teach him all these things, like how to move around the
kitchen, and I teach him how to hem up clothes, and how to make
a simple bread pudding, and you have people would say these is not
t'ings you supposed to teach a little boy – is not so you raise boy
pickney. But chu! What them know? Man supposed to able to keep
house himself, and Gavin learning all these things I teach him. He
really ain't so bad.* Miss Betty would open her arms then and
say to the child, "Come here, man." When he ran and jumped
into her embrace, she would hold him tight and say, "There,
there. You too cry cry. Don't you know you mustn't give
Grandma so much trouble. There, there. There, there…" until
he fell asleep.

But reader, there is abuse and then there is abuse. There is
punishment and then there is punishment. I have told you
already how at seven Gavin asked his grandmother how his
momma looked, and she gave him the shoebox with the
picture in it. It took Miss Betty a whole year before she asked
him back for it… a whole year in which the picture had been
carried everywhere, had been creased and uncreased so many
hundreds of times that it had worn into destruction.

"Where is it?" Miss Betty demanded that day, and Gavin
dared not show her. "Where is it?" and then finally, when she
thought of how the boy had now killed his mother twice, she
shouted, "Laaawdavemercy!!" It was the worst beating she
ever gave him, though it ended as always with Gavin in her
lap and she hushing him, "There, there."

But Miss Betty made a decision that night, a spiteful way to
punish the boy forever. She decided she would never tell
Gavin about his parents. Nothing. Not ever. So in all his
growing up, Gavin was never told what kind of person his
mother was, what music she liked, the little things she would
often say, her peculiarities. He was never told, not by Miss

Betty or anyone, of October 1st, 1977 – the day Darren Williams drove up to the house in the middle of a soft downpour, how the rain stopped the very instant he stepped out of the car, and how she, Miss Betty, knew in that moment that her daughter and this man were meant to be. She never told Gavin that the stone necklace in the shoe box was what his father hung around Sylvia's neck like an engagement ring. Miss Betty decided Gavin would never know.

The old woman, of course, would never guess that Gavin's memory was like the universe, always stretching, expanding, inventing new spaces. Years later, when she and the boy are walking in the plazas buying things for Christmas and they see an old white Ford Escort, it is Gavin who remarks, "That's just like the one Dad used to have," causing Miss Betty to stop cold, look at him closely, wondering *How the hell him could know that?*

*

There is something missing from this story. Why is Gavin growing up without a father? What happened to Darren Williams?

To answer this, we must go way back, past the birth, past the marriage, past the Palisadoes and back to Darren's own childhood – a period of great uneventfulness, a singularly unspectacular upbringing.

His was not a typical Jamaican household; it was too absent of sound. Darren had no siblings. There were no games to fight over; no extra servings of breadfruit or chicken to be jealous of. There was neither any unmarried aunt living with them, nor any abandoned cousin. There was no grandfather living all day in the country of his armchair, occasionally coughing up phlegm and talking about days before the war.

The Williams family were rooted to the house they lived in, a cool one-storey house in the back of a cane community –

"community" perhaps being a little inaccurate since there weren't many people who lived there and the houses were far apart. But Darren's family never thought of moving – that great act of relocation which forces people to pull back the cabinets and the beds and all the furniture which had seemed permanently fixed. And then to find hidden in the dust mementoes of a forgotten time. But this never happened for the Williamses. They stayed where they were, and everything stayed in the dust; nothing to be rediscovered or remembered.

And now the strangest thing of all about Darren's childhood: he never discovered himself. I am speaking of that most profound, guilty and sticky way, in which a teenage boy will find out the texture and the sound and the motions of his own sexuality; will discover the use of fingers and lotion; will discover shame and secrecy and pleasure. This was not part of Darren's growing up.

No siblings, no cousins, no aunts, no grandfather. Never moved houses and never masturbated. How boring! A quiet boy with quiet parents.

Before his mother married, her name was Paulette Cardoza, a slow-witted and stout mulatto woman, proud of her thick black hair and her Spanish last name. How it pained her to marry and change her last name to something so plain and English as "Williams". Double-barrelling was not something done in her day. She often said wistfully to Darren, and only to Darren, "My father name Cardoza, and I could have been a schoolteacher," as if the two things were connected. Poor Paulette, she could never have been a teacher. She never had the brain for it. She spent the great part of her life manning one of the cash registers in her husband's haberdashery store and her incompetence at that task was matched only by her genuine pleasantness. In the early days, her husband would often draw her aside and say "Paulette! Paulette you have to do better. We can't afford to lose money like this. You don't see how the business growing. We need to be professional." But such warnings only made her more nervous and inefficient, and after a while, Mr Williams found out that part of the reason the business was growing was that people had been spreading the word that if they were lucky, the cashier would give them back more change than they deserved. And so Mr Williams reasoned to himself with superb logic, *With Paulette it come in like we have a sale all year round. I won't need to have any other promotion with her working at the machine!*

Mr Williams was a dark Indian man who, every so often, would say very sternly to Darren, "Come and follow me to the store!" But after uprooting the boy from the sanctuary of his house, he would leave him to sit in the shadows all day doing nothing but dodging the store clerks who would reach up and ruffle his hair saying, "Lawd it pretty, eeeh!" so the boy would grow into the habit of hitting people's hands away from his hair. Mr Williams had the desire almost every father possesses, the need to pass down a legacy. But he didn't know how to do it outside of these excursions to the store. Sometimes, and perhaps too often, he repeated this story to Darren, "I start out in this business selling nails. You realize nails is something everybody need? You realize? Good. Well I walk around every-where selling them, and nobody would ever guess that nails can be so heavy until you go 'bout the place with a whole bag of them on your back."

The weight of nails; the dry corners of a store; a grandfather with a Spanish last name; a dream that could never have been. These were the legacies passed down to Darren Williams, legacies which could never move him.

*

What does a quiet child do? How does he pass the time? Darren read. He read voraciously, tirelessly. And yet it was strange, he would never lose himself in the books, it wasn't escapism for him. Simply a thing to do, a puzzle, a race to get from one cover to the next. Most times he did not remember what he read. Would indeed, read the same book again and again without anything being lost. Never tried to comprehend the text, to digest it, just tried to finish. Any kind of book, it was all the same: novels, poetry collections, history books, atlases, encyclopedias, biographies, manuals, biology text books. It didn't matter.

And then, when Darren was twenty-four, he was introduced to Sylvia Thomas, a schoolteacher, just what his mother had wanted to become. In the place when he should have said his name, should have said "Hi, I'm Darren," he heard himself saying, "Love does not begin and end the way we seem to think it does. Love is a battle, love is a war; love is a growing up."

She smiled, "You like James Baldwin. I read him too."

James Baldwin. James Baldwin. The first time Darren ever heard the name. He had read him of course, just had not remembered. When Darren met Sylvia, it was like a circuit-board turned on inside him. Wires began to crackle, lights started to blink. Everything he had read in his life started to surface and become alive. He suddenly had opinions on life and art and history and humanity, and love. And all these things happening at once caused him to gasp, stumble back. Sylvia reached out, grabbed his hand and asked, "You all right, man?"

"Y-yes. I-I'm okay... I'm... I'm Darren. Darren Williams." And he really was okay; just slightly in love. Slightly found – the realization dawning on him that before that moment, for his whole life, he had been lost.

A year later, he took her to the Palisadoes and soon after they were married. You know what happened on their wedding night. You also know what happened nine months after. So tell me, how does a man love his first son, his first son borne to him by the woman whom he gave the gift of his virginity, the woman whom he adores?

He will love that son utterly.

And tell me, how does a man hate the person who killed his first wife, the woman who, in his heart, he would have died for?

He will hate that person utterly.

So what happens when the first son and the wife's killer are one and the same person? It's a simple equation: the love and the hate will cancel each other perfectly. The man will look on his son without a trace of emotion. He will not hate him. He will not love him. His apathy will be utter.

On the day of Sylvia's funeral, Darren went to the barber early and shaved his head completely. He took the hair with him to the graveside, and when the minister said ashes to ashes, dust to dust, Darren threw the cropped hair on top of the coffin and turned around to leave. The ceremony wasn't over, but he had had enough. And on his way out, the little baby Gavin, who he had been holding in his arms, slipped from his embrace. Or maybe he did not slip. Maybe the father just didn't care to hold him any longer and so let go. The result is the same either way, the child fell and hit his head against a stone. It never seemed as if Darren realized or cared, because he did not stop. He walked all the way out, into his Ford Escort and drove off. And that was the last time Darren ever held his son.

4.

The constant voice of Miss Betty that Gavin carries in his head goes something like this:

Make sure you always tidy. Brush you teeth, comb you hair. Make sure no wax in your ears. Clean out de matter from you eyes. Be a good Christian boy. Never let anybody see you spit. Don't belch in public, that is bad manners. Don't shout. I don't raise you as no hooligan – don't act like one. I don't raise you as no ghetto-boy – don't act like one. Always say please and thank you. Make sure you shirt tucked in to you pants, I don't care if is shorts you wearing. Cleanliness is next to Godliness. Neatness is next to Godliness. Good manners is next to Godliness.

Don't whistle in front of me – you want me to box out you teeth? Turn the other cheek. Don't fight. Don't roll your eyes – them will stuck in the back of your head make you only see inside you own body. Don't crick your fingers or you toes – it will make them fat and ugly looking. Don't drink too much sweet drinks – that is bad manners. Never you ask for more. That is bad manners. Don't scratch youself in public, even when mosquito bite you. Always use knife and fork. Always spread a napkin in you lap. Always pray before you eat. Even if is just little sweetie you eating, always pray. Don't talk to Miss Jackson's son – dat boy is the devil himself. Don't talk to Miss Jackson's niece – dat girl too big for her age. Miss Jackson is a whore – but don't tell her I tell you that or I lace you backside from here till tomorrow.

Study you books, I not raising no dunce. Don't read all them books, it will mad you.

Gavin at school was always different from the other children. A boy who carried napkins in his bag and spread one in his lap whenever he ate. A boy who would beg you for a candy and once he had received it, would clasp his hands and close his eyes and say a long prayer. Really, he was something of a schizophrenic, a boy who walked around with voices in his head. Another child would hit him, and Gavin would clench his fist but then hear a voice say *Turn the other cheek. Don't act like a hooligan.* The child would hit him again hard, and Gavin would hear *You too cry cry, man! Don't cry.* The children would form a circle around him, would laugh, would tease him and he would hear *Turn the other cheek don't act like a hooligan you too cry cry sticks and stones may break your bones but not words – words will never hurt.* And a voice, his own voice which he could not recognize – not then – would ask, *Then why this feel so much like hurt? And why it wrong to cry when I feel to cry so bad?* But the answer came, *You mustn't. You're a young man.* And so he would stand there impotent, trembling, the most pitiful sight in the world.

In Grade Three the teacher, Mrs Cox, wrote the word *REMEMBER* on the blackboard. "Now that's a big word," she said to the class, "anybody know what it is?"

The whole class chorused, "Remember!"

"And anyone can tell me what it means?"

Half a dozen hands shot in the air.

"Yes, Jennifer, you give it a go."

"Miss, is like when something happen long long ago and you still see it."

"Yes! Yes, that's it exactly. Very good, Jennifer. Now anyone remembers anything that happened to them they want to share? Like I remember long, long, long ago when I was small just like all of you and my daddy was a fisherman who used to take us on his boat. We would go out when it was dark, dark, dark, because that is the best time to fish. And sometimes we'd go way out in the sea where you can't see no land and the water had even sharks in it. But I was never afraid, because I was with my daddy." The children laughed, because Mrs Cox was quite a plump woman and of course she seemed ancient to the children, like she was born old and no one could imagine her young and with a daddy. "So now it's your turn," she said turning to them, "is there anything you remember you want to share?"

Almost all the hands shot in the air.

"Yes, Robert..."

"Miss, I remember when it was my birthday and my father give me a new train set!"

"Wow! That's lovely. Yes Marcus..."

"Miss, I remember flying in a plane and when it lift up off the ground this woman behind me scream out and my mummy say is 'cause she too fraidy fraidy and fool." The children laughed, and then suddenly everyone had a memory of being on a plane, even those who had never travelled.

Gavin alone sat in silence. He remembered his grandmother talking to him the day before. And the day before that. And the day before that. He remembered her shouting and he remembered her with a belt. And he wondered, how come all these children smile when they remember things. And so he cast his mind far back, and tried to remember a day before the day before the first day he ever knew, and maybe, he thought, if he could do that, he could find a happy memory. And maybe that evening, he would go home, and he would ask his grandmother how his momma looked and based on what she said he would try to remember. Give him time.

*

In 1951, when Elizabeth Thomas arrived in Kingston from the rural backskirts of Clarendon, carrying with her two pieces – a green suitcase filled with clothes, and a scandal bag with two large yams her father had dug up and given to her as a parting gift – she had wanted to become a nurse. All the men who had left, and had made something of themselves in the city, came back looking proper and clean, decked out, each one of them, in some uniform or the other – army fatigues, police gear, the blue blazers that bank clerks wore. So Elizabeth fancied she'd return one day wearing a white uniform, crisp and starched, matching white shoes and that little silver watch buttoned onto her breast pocket.

The two yams, by the way, turned out to be so bitter Elizabeth had to throw them away, so it must be said that she came into town having no advantage. The year, as noted, was 1951, four decades after the Earthquake and a few months before the Hurricane, so Kingston was all too sure of her strength, of her lights, gridded streets and theatres, getting ready to celebrate her 150th birthday. Elizabeth took a job at an office where a little man, Mr Nelson, and his three assistants did accountancy work. She swept out the office in the morning and typed letters for him during the day. She was saving her money for school and on her lunch break she would often walk down the road to watch the nurses on their way to and from Kingston Public Hospital.

But Elizabeth soon discovered the night. She discovered the club, how a man on a sweet saxophone could pull notes out from right inside of you. She discovered sweat and closed spaces and the pull of drums, and dancing: Oh! How she discovered dancing, how everyone took something, some frustration or some joy and they put it all on the dance-floor like an offering, and everybody was one. She loved to dance, she loved holding her body against a man's, and sometimes later on, when he was undressing her and she him, and they lay on the bed, she saw it as the same dance, because music was still playing in her head, even when she gritted her teeth, bucked her hips, took short breaths and whimpered "Sweet Jeeesus! Sweeet Jeeessus!", it was all just one beautiful dance.

The sceptic will say that the possibility of becoming a nurse ended when Elizabeth became pregnant, especially since, to her great consternation, she had no clue who the father was. Word got back to Clarendon about this disastrous state of affairs, and no word came back. It was as if her father had decided she was no longer the kind of daughter who deserved to be sent messages or two pieces of yam.

But whatever is said about Elizabeth Thomas, at least she was a survivor. She continued to sweep out the office and type up letters and save her money little by little. She even went to night class and did a course in First Aid.

The child was born. Elizabeth gave her the name Sylvia and never once found the space to resent her. Of course she now had to dip into the money she had saved – trips to the doctor, baby clothes and food – but in taking care of a life, Elizabeth's resolve was strengthened. She was going to be a nurse! She continued to save for five years, mopping the floors of that office, wiping it out, making tea for anyone who asked and typing letters during the day. She began to wear that small silver watch clipped to her breast, and when the people at work asked, she said proudly, "Is to remind me. I going to be a nurse."

The tragedy happened on a cool day in February. Elizabeth had just finished mopping the floor and so it was wet. But Mr Nelson, stepping out of the bathroom and walking briskly to his desk as he usually did, managed to lose his balance that morning. When he skidded and cried out there was a whole second when everyone looked up and saw him in the air. Falling. His head split against the edge of his work desk and he crumpled to the floor without a sound. Everyone stood up quickly, everyone too shocked to say anything.

Elizabeth, mop still in her hand, standing a few feet away, looked down on Mr Nelson and then looked up. She caught the gaze of the other office workers, and it seemed to her for a while each one was looking on the nurse's watch buttoned to her chest, looking to her for direction. Elizabeth flung down the mop, remembered the first rule in First Aid, and shouted, "Everybody calm down! Everybody calm down!

Everybodyjustcalmdown!" And fourteen hours later, she woke up.

It was dark. She was in the hospital. One of the office workers was standing by the side of the bed and smiled when she opened her eyes. "Oh. I just come from visiting Mr Nelson. Thought I would see how you was."

"What happen," Elizabeth asked, still groggy, "what happen to Mr Nelson?"

The young man smiled. "Him was unconscious for a long time. They say him have a concussion and him get a nasty cut. You need to see him," he laughed, "Them wrap him head up like them Egyptian mummy. Mister Nelson not going to be at work for this week at least... Like we get a little break."

"Chu man! How you can say a thing like that..."

"I know, I know. I taking bad things make joke."

Elizabeth shook her head. "At least him okay... I just feel kinda shame. Imagine all I could do was scream out like a idiot."

The office worker looked at her curiously. "Scream?"

Elizabeth looked back at him. "When I was shouting at all of you to calm down."

"When that was?"

Elizabeth didn't understand. "Right after Mr Nelson drop! Me. Shouting at everybody. You don't remember?"

The young man frowned. "Nothing like that did happen..." he almost whispered. "Look like you take one look at the blood and you faint."

"But..."

"When the ambulance come they take you and Mr Nelson up the same time. You never make a sound... well, except the big boof when you hit the ground." He smiled and then felt apologetic. "Is just now you waking back up."

"But... but I don't remember..." And then she was silent. Elizabeth knew he was telling the truth. She with her big ambition of wearing a white uniform, white cap and white shoes. Administering injections. Checking people's blood pressure. Cleaning cuts. Helping out doctors in surgery. She same one who wanted to become big big nurse had to finally admit what had always been a stumbling block: from she was a little girl, she fainted at the sight of blood.

5.

Draw a Venn diagram – a box, and inside of that box, a few circles, and within those circles, even smaller circles. This is how we learn about sets and subsets; we learn that every group is inside a larger group, and also the converse, that inside every large group, there are smaller groups. Take, for instance, food: within that you have fruits, within that you have citrus, and within that you have oranges, all different kinds of oranges.

Or to use another example – Jamaica: within that you have Kingston, within that you have Vineyard Town, and within that you have all different kinds of small communities. The community of old women for instance: those shameless hypocrites who meet each day by their hedges to spread gossip and scandal about each other. The ever-changing community of stray dogs that shit in the roads and end up being killed by fast cars, leading one madman to declare over one of these roadkills, "Verily, I say unto you, mongrels, if you live by de sword, oonoo will dead by de sword. And if you live by de road, oonoo go dead by de road too."

So yes, there was a "community" of mad people. Only two of them. The aforementioned man who loved to speak biblically, a trait which earned him the name Elijah: though unlike the Old Testament prophet this squat little man would prophesy about things that needed no prophesying about. The point about dogs dying on the road, for instance, was moot in a country that had more stray mongrels than sidewalks or fences, where cars seemed to be their only natural predator, the only things able to stop what was obviously a strategic plan to breed and populate at such a rate that they could soon demand political power. The sight of a morning roadkill in such a country simply becomes part of the landscape.

The second "mad person" was an elderly woman who had been a receptionist before she lost her mind. She spoke the Queen's English and had the unsettling ability to remember people's names. "Good morning, Mrs Brown, and how are you this morning?" she would ask approaching a car window. But then there was the rare occasion when someone didn't give her the money she begged so nicely for. In these instances she would drop the fancy talk, lift up her skirt and curse every expletive she had ever come across in her life; it seemed that she had come across quite a few. But these two proper-speaking mad people made the residents of Vineyard Town quite proud, and they boasted to anyone who would listen, "Is we have de most educated mad people in Jamaica!"

There was also in Vineyard Town a community of young women who set out before sunrise each day to become nurses or gas attendants or to sweep out offices or to type letters for their corporate executive bosses. And a community of men who did electrical work, and plumbing and construction, who drank white rum by the pubs as they slapped down dominoes. And a community of the idle unemployed; and a small community of college students; and now, finally, the most important group: the community of boys. Most important, not because it is their sounds that dominate the street; not because it is their mischief that adds flavour and life; not because it is their names which are always shouted into the evenings: *Peter, Jeremy! Get you ass inside now!* But rather, because they are the storytellers. They are the ones who walk from house to house, and gather from the insides and the outsides and corners of each one, its own tale; they laugh over these stories, add on to them, tell them again and again. They are the ones who hide behind lightpoles whenever Tanya Ellis is stepping out of a taxi, and shout out "Slut!", because they have heard that every boy past the age of sixteen has worn proudly at the base of his penis the moist red circular stamp of Tanya's lipstick. They are the ones who duck by number 15 and holler, "Miss Lazarus, mind you wig drop off!" They, the story-tellers, are always the ones who have the authority to look on just about any jackman or woman, and tell them exactly who they are.

The boys of Vineyard Town are: Dwight, the unquestioned leader, tall for his thirteen years, long limbs and long fingers that would have looked elegant if your eyes were not drawn away from them and to the scars which sprouted new on his arms and face almost every day. He was as much the leader because of these "badges" as for the authority with which he used curse words; he alone, amongst the boys, had learned to say the words "fuck" and "shit" with all the naturalness and ease of a grown man at a construction site. Other boys were impressed and tried to imitate him. There were the twins, Keron and Kwame, both left-handed, but the best cricket batters around. Johnny, the most mischievous, famous for his trick of making his eyeballs go in two completely different directions. Fire, a handsome dread-locks who was always the victim of some mastermind plan that would have him eating pork without knowing it.

And Gavin... is Gavin a part of this community? He is a boy and he is from Vineyard Town – is that qualification enough?

We will see. Let us follow all six boys – Dwight, Keron, Kwame, Johnny, Fire and Gavin – to Kingston Harbour.

It is the summer of 1992, the year it became official that Jamaican Dancehall was serious. Serious and biblical. No longer a place for joking or making fun. Dancehall was for prophecy. Buju Banton began his rise as the voice of Jamaica; fitting really, because he had grown up in Salt Lane, so who else to sing and prophesy on this whole business of sucking salt if not him? Those who went out to party learnt to dance with a terrible face, a screwed up and angry face, 'cause if you smiled it would look all wrong. So now you'd have a man alone, in the middle of the dance floor, Heineken bottle in hand, eyes closed, pennying the lyrics, *Woe, be unto dem – he who rise against poor people shall perish inna de end*, dancing this serious dance 'cause these were serious times.

Imagine these six boys, bandanas tied around their heads, sunglasses, walking this stiff, serious kind of walk that they imagined was how a man was supposed to move, walking determinedly down to the waters as if there were no other mission in the world more important.

But boys are boys, and when they reach the water, what else is there to pretend at? Not with the water and its promise of all of what summer should be. Not with Johnny, who shouts as soon as they reach the stones that border the water, "Last man in love suck pussy…"; there is only a moment's hesitation before each boy decides he is actually not too old to play this game. Shoes are kicked off, bandanas and shades tossed to the side, merinos stripped off, then Splash! Splash! Splash! They dive in, then come up, wiping the salt water out of their eyes, to look back and laugh at the one boy still sitting on the stones, "Gavin, you love suck pussy! Gavin you is a bowcat! Hahaaaa." But they had known that already, because he was always the one who never swam.

The boys splash each other; they play "water war", race, try to dunk each other under. Gavin is comfortable just watching. He likes to sit back under the sun and take it all in, the warm wind, the view. Kingston Harbour is his favourite spot in the world. He once read in a newspaper article the details of how the harbour was formed, and though most would find this kind of information boring he was completely fascinated: how it was the Hope River would take with it little particles on its way out to the sea. How the particles built up over thousands of years to form the five miles of the Palisadoes Strip, as if this was Kingston's long arm reaching out to hug a little piece of the Caribbean Sea unto itself. One of the largest natural harbours in the world, that's what he read.

Gavin loves the waterfront because it is here he can look out and forget the present. And this forgetting is really an act of memory, a time when he can go all the way back. He tries to remember everything; himself as a little boy, himself as a baby. At times he will even try to remember being in his mother's womb; he will try to remember his parents. And give him time. Give him time and it will all come back.

After almost an hour, Dwight is the first to swim back and lift himself out of the water, his shorts almost dropping off, the white underwear showing, his chest and stomach so smooth in sharp contrast to his scarred hands, and him, unaware of – or perhaps unconcerned with – this budding masculinity. Gavin is almost nervous around Dwight. The long-limbed boy sits down on a rock, flashes his hands out playfully so Gavin is sprayed with drops of salt water. Dwight laughs, "Fuck! You 'fraid o' water?"

"No."

"So how you always come down here and you never ever swim?"

Gavin tries to smile, "I'm all right."

Dwight laughs again. "My yout', me never ask if you was all right. Fuck! You think me love man? Me ask why you don't swim..."

Gavin felt something like a stone rise up to his throat and was about to stammer out an answer, but he was saved because by then all the other boys had emerged out of the harbour. Fire, his dreadlocks dripping with water, shouted, "Watch dis now!" and sailed a pebble across the water; it bounced four times before sinking. The display stole Dwight's attention and he sprang to his feet, picked up a pebble and tried to outdo Fire, skipping his own stone across. It only skipped three times, so he tried again, and then again. And soon, the other boys had picked up stones and joined in the competition.

Listen, there is a physics behind skipping stones, a science that will calculate diameter, mass, tilt, velocity, the angle of attack, the density of the water. Good "skippers" always know this science – perhaps not its numbers or its divisions or its multiplications. But they know it – the action that is necessary to produce good results, how to spread the feet, how to arc the hand, how to flick the wrist in a way that gives the stone spin, when to release and at what general angle.

And there is another kind of person who does not understand this science, neither the theory nor the practical, neither the calculation nor the execution. A kind of person who will watch Dwight or Fire approach the water like a golfer coming to tee, the right arm raised across his chest, the swing, the beautiful arc, the stone released and bouncing creating a kind of grammatical miracle... ellipses spread across the water; there is a kind of person who watching all of this, will not see the science, but the art, the beauty of it. Gavin was such a person: a flat-footed and overweight boy who could not ride bicycles himself but who would watch, loved the exhibitionism when the other children would take their hands off the handlebar and stand, or when they lifted their front wheels when flying over speed bumps. Gavin was the kind of person who could not skip stones but who was content just watching. So you can imagine the terror when Dwight says meanly, "Hey, fat coolie bwoy! Your turn!"

"My turn for what? No man, I all right."

"I tell you already, I never ask if you all right. I telling you that is your turn!" The five boys fold their arms and wait, grinning. Gavin is afraid.

A complete list of phobias would probably be a dictionary of its own. Some of them you would never imagine really exist – like the fear of teenagers (ephibiphobia), or the fear of lake water (limnophobia), and there is even the fear of stones (lithophobia). Defeated, Gavin searches through the rock pile, makes his selection barely aware that it is too round, too heavy – but what difference would even the most perfect stone make? He braces himself, tosses it out, something like a cricket fielder throwing back the ball to the bowler, straight up in the air, before it begins its descent. The stone goes *plonk!* in the water and sinks.

The five boys behind him cannot contain themselves. They slap their knees, bend over and laugh loud and raucous from their bellies. A new story is recorded. It is Keron, one of the twins, who finally declares as he takes a breath and wipes away the tears, "Gavin! You throw like one little gyal!" Shameful that, coming from a leftie who always looked a little strange himself when skipping stones or even when writing. But it is Dwight who corrects Keron, "No, my yout'. Gavin don't throw like a little gyal. Him throw like a big battyman!"

*

Draw a Venn diagram – a box, and inside of that box, a few circles, and within those circles, even smaller circles. Now, fill the spheres with letters – write them in: *a, b, c, d*... all except for one. Leave the letter *z* in the box, but outside of any of the circles. This is a person like Gavin, a person who grows up, and while the simple fact of existing must mean that he belongs to the universe, which group within that universe is he anchored to? Where is his tribe?

6.

Each life is filled with its own peculiarities. Its own absurdities. Why, for instance am I, a professor of Mathematics through and through, engaged in the literary act of telling you a story? One theory says every tale is the story of the person telling it. That every character is only a mask. I would like to comment on that. I want to object strenuously. I am not Gavin. This is not my story. It is only my telling. Furthermore, I object to the theory of "all" and "every". Hardly anything is ever one hundred percent. That all writing is autobiography is ridiculous. There are similarities of course. But aren't there always?

This is Gavin's story, and some of the absurdities in his life are as follows: the smell of a lit coil of mosquito destroyer could make him lose an erection. When he was sixteen he was ready to lose his virginity to a pretty girl from Portmore. Latetia Goldbourne, a bright girl in Lower Six, had told him her parents were away, so the house was free for the night. This was completely true, although she made it seem that on another night soon the parents would return which wasn't true. Latetia never knew her father, and her mother had flown off to New Jersey a year and a half ago. The daughter was left in Jamaica to live on her own though the mother did send money and other supplies regularly. Latetia had now grown into the habit of inviting boys over, trying to fill the space of the otherwise empty house.

But Latetia's house was in Portmore. Portmore was a large community surrounded on almost every side by swamp – stagnant water, thick and green and harbouring both crocodiles and mosquitoes. It seemed at times the two species were competing for the title of "Most Vicious". In that year there was a popular high school joke: how do you keep a mosquito out of a Portmore house? You lock the gate. Portmore mosquitoes really did seem more fierce and large than others on the island. So that night, when Latetia pulled Gavin into her bedroom, unbuttoning his shirt in the process, he found lit two coils of mosquito destroyer, causing him to fumble, draw his pants back up and excuse himself awkwardly. Mosquito destroyer = impotence; at least that's what he told her.

Another absurdity of his life: he liked his hot dog with peanut butter spread on the buns. And another: he favoured the colour yellow. Would buy bright yellow clothes, jeans and shoes, and wear these proudly. This is one of the reasons I can remember the first time I ever met Gavin. It was the semester I started teaching at the university. It was the middle of the term and at least half my students could not grasp how to do a partial differential equation. It didn't make sense to move on. So I spent the class reviewing the topic. Halfway through the class, the front door of the lecture hall squeaked open. I have taught now for a few years at the university and it is my firm belief that the maintenance department never oils any of the doors, so when they open, they open loudly and the class is forced to stop. It made it worse that this interruption came from the front of the class, not the backdoor where it is much more polite for a student to enter after the class has begun. In stepped Gavin, bright yellow jeans, bright yellow sandals. A large knapsack over his back. Growing into his height at the time, more stocky than fat. Fiercely handsome. He looked up at the class, and then he looked at me. Baffled. He looked at the class again, then at me.

"Yes sir, might we be of any assistance?" I said in my most bastardly tone. The class snickered. Gavin seemed to pay it no mind. He looked at me again, confused. "Sir, may I help you please?" I repeated, "We are in the middle of a class."

"This isn't *History of the Caribbean*," he said. More a statement than a question.

I was tempted to say something harsh again. The classes had switched lecture theatres from the second week, the *History of the Caribbean* group needing much more room than *Introduction to Mathematics*. The kind of student who only deigns to find out where his class is actually located that late in the semester, is the kind of student the university can do without, the kind of student who will drop out in short order in any case. I was annoyed, but still I answered gently. "You'll find them in the Interfaculty Lecture Theatre."

Gavin nodded and left without saying another word. He made his way across campus and this time entered the lecture theatre correctly, from the back, easing the door open softly and sitting down in the background with a minimum of fuss. The truth, actually, is that it didn't matter. The class was in the middle of an obviously lively debate. Students were protesting something about Arawaks and Caribs, while the professor smiled softly, waiting for quiet. Gavin knew about Arawak Indians and their enemies the Caribs. It was the history you learned even in primary school. The Arawaks were a peace-loving tribe while the Caribs were a war-mongering set of Indians. The Caribs were also cannibals, and even before Christopher Columbus and the Spaniards came to finish the deed, these native Indians had already weakened the Arawak people.

The class uproar finally subsided and the lecturer continued his point. "Look guys. When I say there was no such thing as 'Arawaks' and 'Caribs' I'm talking about the labels. We're finding out now that there was no actual difference between the two tribes. It was one set of people. Europeans simply called the 'Indians' who surrendered one thing, and the 'Indians' who put up a fight they called another. You do realize how 'Indian' is another unfortunate label we carry from that great mistake in history. Anyway, it was all typical European propaganda. Even the bit about Caribs being cannibalistic. Cannibalism is one of the single biggest lies Europe used to justify their colonial expansion. Africans were said to be cannibals, and the 'Arawaks' who were more aggressive were called cannibals too, and given their own name, which you know: 'Caribs'. And to this day we believe that lie. But I tell you something," the professor smiled, "I'm glad they named this region after the people who dared to put up a fight."

The class laughed. They were all listening spellbound. Even Gavin was hanging on to every word. He'd never heard history like this in high school. He never knew history was a thing you could challenge, revise, correct. He was ready to hear more, but that was not to be. The professor looked on his watch and announced, "I guess we will pick up in our next class." Students immediately started to get up out of their seats noisily, packing up their books and exiting while others made their way to the front of the class to ask their lecturer questions. The professor shouted over the din, "Remember to read Chapter 6 and your essays are due next week!" A few choruses of "Yes sir," and in short time the room was empty, just the small queue of students lined up before the professor.

Gavin joined the line. The students in front of him wanted to know when the results for the mid-semester exam would be posted. They wanted to know how long the essay had to be, and did it have to be typed, and would they count every single word? Typical student questions. Gavin waited for his turn. Finally, he stepped in front of the professor. Dr Darren Williams looked down on his son, recognized him and stood with his mouth open, not making a sound. Stupidly, instinctively, Darren looked on his watch. He was trying to account for the time. He was trying to add up the years. Could he really have a son old enough to be in college? Was it that long ago that Sylvia died? Sylvia, distanced now to a lonely event in history, like Caribs and Arawaks. She never felt like history to him. And as he stood there, trying to count the years, Gavin ran past him. It was then that Darren tried to reach for him. To finally touch his son again. Missed.

The boy found his way back home. He was only fifteen. Not a university student. He had skipped school in order to see his father. He lurked in the background of that class, and observed the man he had never had the chance to call "Dad". He witnessed the wry smile, the quiet brilliance. Gavin saw how an entire lecture hall could grow quiet without him calling for it, just because they wanted to hear what he would say next, what new thing would tumble out of his mouth so they could scramble for it and own it for themselves.

When Gavin ran past his father, it was not histrionics. The only person he was angry with was himself. He wondered suddenly if he was the kind of son Darren would approve of? The kind of child Darren could ever be proud of? And he was thinking that a professor is not the kind of man who had time to waste. And Gavin thought of how he was standing in front of this man, with absolutely nothing to say, and how the man checked his watch because he had somewhere to go. And Gavin felt foolish, wanting suddenly to fall into the background again, become inconspicuous.

7.

People are forever growing up and away. When Kwame and Keron were fifteen their parents bought a house in Mona, so the family moved. Soon after, Johnny migrated to Canada where rumour had it he began doing extremely well in school, which was a surprise, because Johnny was such a troublemaker that teachers were always putting him in the back of the class or outside. Fire also migrated, to Antigua, and people said his mother was fool-fool, because why would she leave one island only to go to a next one? It couldn't be that much better.

By the time Gavin was eighteen, only he and Dwight were left. Gavin had shed most of his baby fat and had started working as a flight attendant. He had done average in his high school exams, got good enough grades but didn't have the imagination – not yet – to do college. It was 1997, and one day while walking to the bus stop, a woman old enough to be his mother grabbed his arm, looked in his face incredulously and declared, "You're beautiful! Absolutely beautiful! You should be a model or work on one of those airlines or be a stripper!" She laughed. "I'm sorry. Don't mind me."

He was polite, smiled and said thanks, but when she left, he weighed his options and decided there really was nothing to lose. He went into the *Air Jamaica* office and then to a modelling agency in New Kingston. They both offered him contracts but he decided to work on the airline. He was still a young man who didn't belong, so the plane was for him not so much a sign as a meaning, a place from which he could search the world for the person to whom he had always been a shadow. Search the world for his tribe.

Dwight, on his part, learnt how to hustle, to pick up odd jobs on construction sites, weekend work at the supermarket;

for two weeks he even sold newspapers. And when he wasn't working he blended easily into the company of the rum-bar drinkers or he sat on the sidewalk all night with only the amber glow of his cigarette to declare his presence. He would sit there contemplating God knows what, and sometimes he asked the occasional late night passer-by for money, as if he were a total stranger to them.

This is how he came upon Gavin one night – Gavin, tired, returning late from work, walking only mechanically, because he had basically fallen asleep already, so he wasn't paying attention to his surroundings, hadn't seen the glow of Dwight's cigarette. "Beg you a bills nuh my yout'!" delivered in a growl that made Gavin panic for a second.

"You frighten me there," he said when he realized who it was.

Dwight never replied; the smell of tobacco lingered between them. Then suddenly, as if to remind Gavin of the question, "Beg you a bills."

Gavin was annoyed, too tired to deal with yet another beggar. The country was too full of them and he didn't expect it from someone he had grown up with. He sucked his teeth, "I don't have any money, man."

"You have money. Don't tell lie. You coming from work."

And he really did have money stuffed in the bottom of his pocket, but who was Dwight to tell him whether he was lying or not. What right did any beggar have to his money, especially one from Vineyard Town, who couldn't claim to have had a harder life. "I say I don't got no money. I don't have no bills to give you."

Dwight stood directly in front of Gavin. "So if you empty you pockets now I not go see no money. Is that you saying?"

"That's what I saying."

"That's what you really saying?" Stepping even closer.

134

Pause.

Let me digress and tell you a true story. In their run-up to the 1998 World Cup, the Jamaican team played a match in a South American country that shall remain nameless; nameless, but you know South America and their football. Football is passion and it is a big broad banner that is raised, while everyone watches teary-eyed, their right hands clasped over their chests. A thing worth dying for. So when the Jamaican team landed they were greeted by a country whose people were willing to stay up outside the hotel all night, keeping the foreign team awake, booing them. The Jamaicans had to be followed around by bodyguards and each man called home and asked his mother to pray for him. It was tension, a time bomb waiting to explode, and it finally did in the actual match when a Jamaican was kicked down, and another one shoved. The crowd began to celebrate this onslaught, things looked like falling apart, and when the camera focused, there they were, five Jamaican players running the length of the outskirts of the field, bent over, their eyes glued to the ground and their right arms outstretched. The international reporters wondered what kind of dance is this? What kind of ritual? But every Jamaican who watched put their heads in their hands for shame, because they understood; the players were angry and were searching for stones.

Gavin, afraid, cannot run the length of a football field. Instead, he looks inside of himself, draws for the hardest words which are still there, lodged in his centre, the words shouted at his recently birthed self, the words which have remained all these years, pronouncing themselves over his life again and again. He takes these words and throws them at the beggar in front of him, "Lawdhavemercyfuckyou!"

He tries to push past, but the enraged Dwight grabs him by the arm. Gavin shakes off the hand. Dwight, ready to fight, grabs him again, ends up holding Gavin by the waist. They look at each other – two bulls, red-eyed and huffing, hooves scraping the earth – and they look at each other and they look at each other and suddenly, something melts between the two of them, and there is something different in the way Dwight is holding on to Gavin and they look at each other. In a voice that has lost all of its growl, Dwight only manages to say, "Gavin..." who would have in turn responded "Dwight..." if there wasn't something like a solid bubble expanding in his throat right then. Years later, he will think if only he had managed to get that word out, something else would have happened that night. But right then, right now, there is only silence. A silence in which Gavin considers a lie he told to a pretty girl from Portmore a year before, something about the scent of mosquito destroyers and his sudden lack of interest. A silence in which Dwight's lips continue to move, forming words but making no sound – an act of control, as if by keeping his lips busy with words and syllables, they will not be drawn to the mouth they so desperately want to reach right now. And so it is true, if Gavin had responded "Dwight", the lips across from his would have indeed lost control, and something else would have happened.

Eventually, Dwight allows his hands to fall away from Gavin, and after a moment, in a voice that is desperately trying to find back its menace, says, "Just walk on yaaah. Just walk."

Gavin obeys. His eyes completely closed, he walks all the way home, suddenly afraid of himself.

Here is a bit of flawed logic: for everything that exists, there is a word. If there is not a word for something, then it stands to reason the thing does not exist. But what has Gavin always been afraid of? What is the fear of stones – no, the fear of being stoned? What is it called, this expectancy some men carry in their backs that there are people out there, so righteous and exact in their hatred that they will pick up a stone and fling it after us – an accusation, a punishment, a curse for not fitting in, for not belonging to some tribe they have decided all men must belong to. Is there a name for the premonition lurking in our blood that one day friends will turn their backs and families will disown us? Language is limited. There is no single word for such a thing, but such a thing does exist.

*

On July 28th 1999, Miss Betty had a massive stroke and died. Her obituary, which appeared in the *Gleaner*, read:

> *Elizabeth Thomas, age 67, of Vineyard Town, died on 28/07/99 leaving grandson Gavin and other friends and relatives. Funeral service will be held on August 7th 1999 at the Hopewell Chapel, Vineyard Town. Interment follows at Meadowrest Memorial. Please, no floral tributes.*

*

Tragedy is a lonely thing. It cannot stand alone. The saying goes that it always comes in threes. But maybe, if life cannot manage a triple onslaught of bad tidings it will settle on just the pair. A few weeks after Miss Betty's death, Darren Williams also died. The University issued the following press release in all the newspapers:

> **University Professor Passes**
>
> *Dr Darren Williams, Reader in the Department of History at the University of the West Indies, and author of the seminal work, 'Something Old, Something New: Colonial Representations in 20th Century Jamaican Households' and the essay, 'Furniture as Historical Text', died on Saturday August 21st, 1999 after a brief illness.*
>
> *Williams received his first degree from UWI in 1982. He was a Commonwealth Scholar and went on to do his doctoral thesis at*

the University of Toronto in Canada. Dr Williams has been one of Jamaica's most accomplished scholars. His research focused on modern archaeology, post-coloniality and also Indo-Caribbean culture.

Though a quiet man, Dr Williams's work spoke loudly, eloquently and in volumes. He shall be missed. The university extends its condolences to the parents of Darren Williams who survive him.

And what of the child? At his father's memorial service, Gavin sat between his two grandparents. He was not a complete stranger to them. Some Saturdays he had followed Miss Betty to the haberdashery where once a month she collected a cheque. Paulette would sometimes walk over and ask Miss Betty, "And how he getting along in school?" as if he wasn't there to answer for himself, and indeed it was Miss Betty who would answer, one grandmother to another, "Him getting on quite fine. You know I'm stern with him."

Mrs Williams would frown but still say "Good, good," and then as if to apologize directly to Gavin, "You know your daddy. He off doing all kinds of work and studies. It soon mad him."

After the funeral, old Mr Williams patted Gavin on the shoulder and said, "Come, come" and with those two words, Gavin understood that he had a new home. The three of them went into the Morris Oxford, a car Mr Williams had owned for almost three decades, because while he had done well in business he was never the kind of man to show it off in new cars or new houses. They drove to that one-storey house behind the cane where the Williamses still lived and when they reached it, Paulette took Gavin by the hand and said, "Follow me."

She took him into Darren's bedroom. There wasn't really a bed in it, only a small cot. The walls were lined with bookcases, so many books Gavin had never seen in one place except a library: and in a way that's exactly what this was, a library, books rising from the ground up to the ceiling, double stacked, arranged alphabetically and packed so tightly there was no air in between them.

"This is the kind of man you daddy was," Paulette offered, looking around. "I guess these is all yours now. You will have the most use of it."

One day, Gavin really will find the use of it; one day he will be moved by this heritage his father has left him, but that will take time. There are things to work out. But what will help dear reader, is that one day, many years from now, Gavin will find in one of the boxes stuffed on these shelves a picture: October 1st, 1977, Darren and Sylvia picnicking by an aqueduct, comfortable, in love, a stone necklace resting between her breasts. And right beneath that picture, a series of poems written to him in the months before he was born; a map found, crumbs restored, as if Darren had indeed finally made his way back.

*

It is the simple things that often fascinate me. While I was in college and still writing my dissertation, it was fashionable to be fascinated by complicated things like Fermat's Last Theorem – that there was no solution for the equation $X^n + Y^n = Z^n$ where 'n' was greater than 3. A problem so difficult, for a moment it had seemed the new millennium would have dawned without the proof being found. But three hundred and fifty years of work finally paid off, and it was cracked.

The truth is, Fermat's Last Theorem never moved me. Not even the legend that Fermat himself had found the proof, scribbled it on some loose page as he did with all his formulas, and how that page must have been swept out with the rubbish, lost forever. And just to think that this problem might be so simple, so easy it could fit on a little piece of paper, yet it had eluded mathematicians for hundreds and hundreds of years. But not even then was I honestly moved. And yet I am amazed by obvious things; for instance, how the figure at the end of any equation can be arrived at by a million million million other calculations. So $7 + 6 + 8 + 1 = 22$. But so is $2 + 10 + 10$, and so is $515.9 / 23.45$. All equalling 22. And it is strange, isn't it, how different people will live their separate lives in their separate worlds and end up being so similar. Listen, this is not my story, it is only my telling. And yet...

The second time I saw Gavin Williams was at the memorial service for his father. It took some time before I remembered him as the boy who interrupted my class some five years before, wearing bright yellow jeans. There was a third time I would meet him. And then a fourth, and one day we would become friends. But the second time was at the funeral.

I went because Dr Williams was well regarded in the university community. He had had an encyclopaedic mind and that rare gift, that wonderful scope of knowledge, to be able to have a good conversation with just about anyone on just about anything. So when he died there was a sense of sadness, a feeling that something important was subtracted from the world.

I did not know him well. I had never been invited to the house behind the cane. No one was. I never talked with him about personal things, like how he grew up. Like how I grew up. Which high school he went to. He did not know the trivia of my life. I did not know the trivia of his. But still, at the service, I was taken aback by the fact of a son. Williams with his broad scholar's mind had just never seemed the type for messy things like sex and procreation; certainly not one given to family. So then, where did this fully-grown son come from?

And then to see the boy, beautiful boy, sitting there in the pews like stone, as if he himself could not appreciate he had a father, much less one that was dead. Looking on him, I thought again how a million million calculations can arrive at the same end. I thought that this boy was reminding me of me. I thought about the word that doesn't exist to describe the fear of stone.

The pastor said "Amen." Mrs Williams held the urn to her chest and marched solemnly towards the open church doors, the rest of us standing and waiting in the pews. I wondered briefly if when she reached the door, there would be a crowd of mourners ready to blow black bubbles in the air. And then all at once I had the urge to hug Gavin, this boy who I never knew, but who I already knew. I looked around to where he was standing. His grandfather patted him on the shoulder, said "Come, come." He stopped where I was standing, still in the pews. Looked up. I bit my lips. Kept my hands in my pocket. Nodded. He walked past. And this all happened two years before we met.

Calabash, Broken

1.

Is like he never understood boundaries or walls. Is like he never knew that to get from one room to another you had to find the door, open it, step through it. He always had the mind to just float through walls, like they wasn't even there; but people will stare if you do something crazy like that. They might even scream. They will think you odd. Think you is a duppy.

A duppy who have no consciousness of concrete and walls and doors and boundaries and the things that separate us; a duppy who see the world as one open field. That's what he was like. You would be having dinner with lots of people and the talk is about politics, then all of a sudden he get up and looking to his mother across the table, and shout out, "Mummy! Mummy! I want to doo-doo! I need to doo-doo!" And everybody fork freeze in their hands and nobody even blinking and his mother closing her eyes tight tight like she wishing this was another bad dream and him know that him do it again; his words come out like a man floating through walls. His words always crossing boundaries they wasn't supposed to.

Now somebody would hold Miss Gloria's hands. Her eyes still shut tight, but a tear squeeze its way out. She shake her head stiffly. "Why at sixteen him can't learn yet, eeh? Why!"

2.

The day Mary's boyfriend left she didn't cry, because it was raining. What the sense in tears when the world so full of water already? She only stand up there in the middle of the great, grey world where everything – the trees, the houses, the cars – was flickering between the lightning as if it was a black and white TV show and the picture not so good.

She stood up under all that water, her face fallen, her shoulders drooping and the rain beating down like young drummers. Wasn't no healing in that rain neither, no "Lay down your burdens down by the riverside", no "Dip them in the healing stream", no "Sailing across Jordan". It was just water and water, her poor brain growing soft like water.

3.

... and because he forgot boundaries and walls, he would also forget the order of things. Like coming out of the bath one Tuesday, he put on a T-shirt without drying off. Then he forgot to put on underwear or shorts.

He climbed up on to his bed and picked up two calabash rattles, his favourite toys. You could make music with them and don't have to worry about keys and notes, octaves and sharps, rules, you never have to worry about "eedyat" rules. Just had to shake it, *shakashak! shakashakashak!*

Bouncing on the bed now: Jump *shakashaka*, jump-*shakashaka*, jump*shakashaka*. He grew hard.

His erect penis was something that frightened him. Him not telling nobody, but for two years him watching and getting worried about it, how it could all of a sudden get hard and ugly-looking, how with each year it was swelling bigger and bigger.

Jump, *shakashaka*. His member hitting him against his belly. Jump, *shakashaka*. Then is jump him jump straight off the bed – *shakashaka* – walking out the room and down the stairs – *shakashaka* – because he now decide to tell his mother, his mother who right then was talking to the new helper; the new helper who look up and almost drop down from shock. To get his mother's attention, him hitting her on the shoulder, "Mummy! Look on my peepee!"

Miss Gloria look and feel shame. Shame because of the thing she see; shame because is pride she think she hearing in the boy's voice. "Jesus saviour pilot me!" she whisper.

Pilot! Pilot! Now him start thinking of fly-cross-the-sky pilot! Airplanes. Being up there like a bird, imagine that! Him stretch him hands out like wings, running around the room, butt-naked and stiff, zooooooom zooooooooom *shakashaka*!

"Philip! Philip! Stop that."

Him never take her on. The rattles in his hand sound like an airplane engine to him; the running about making him feel excited. Is all so much fun. Zooooooooom *shakashaka*.

"Philip!" Miss Gloria get up to grab him, but is out him run out of the room. She stumble behind him, cursing. Him run through rooms, run upstairs, run through the front door. She vex and panicking and screaming, "Philip *stop!*"

But he don't understand that she serious. Him think she playing with him again, finally loving him again. Him about to run into the road. She catch up and drag him by the shirt cuff. Him out of breath, look up smiling. "Mummy! You catch me!"

Waaap! Straight 'cross him face. His penis went limp.

"Why you must do this to me, eeeh boy?"

She grab the two calabash rattles and slam them on the ground. One cracked open, red seeds pouring out.

144

4.

Is not drown Mary was trying to drown herself. Well, not really.

Remember the boyfriend left. Then the rain stopped. Now she always find herself walking past water and looking in; always the water would seem to open its doors and invite her, singing, "Come just as you are... this is the place where left-over-things rest... when a man reach inside you, take out you heart and fling it 'way careless, when you find youself as hollow as the tinman, this is where you belong."

Many days you would see her in Kingston Harbour, floating belly-up, and if you didn't look close to see her stomach rising and falling, you would think she was a corpse some gunman had dumped into the sea. Is not drown she was trying to drown; is just that when every cell in your body turn itself into sorrow it will want to turn into water next. Out there in Kingston Harbour, she thought she would dissolve, become part of the ocean.

5.

Listen to a myth: living near to the equator, some days will feel like leather. That's if you believe the story that the world is a calabash broken in two and that a great snake has wrapped herself around the centre to hold it together.

Some days if you step outside, lift your head in the wind, you will feel the belly of the snake resting against your cheeks.

6.

Sometimes, Philip just want to stay outside. He would climb up on the gate, don't care that him not a little child any more. The middle of the gate had sunk in deeply from so many years of bearing his weight. He would sit there for hours just looking at the sky.

When you outside, everything is under one roof. The world is wide and without walls. Him feel more comfortable here. As the years go by it harder for him to listen to his mother when she calling him in. Sometimes him pretend him don't hear her, just so he can stay out there for an extra five minutes.

"Philip!" She look outside and see him humming intensely to himself, rocking on the gate.

"Philip!" She could see his whole body tense and him just start to hum louder, rock himself more. *God*, she wonder, *why life have to be like this?* She step outside, all of the old anger in her voice, "Philip, come inside right now!"

"No!"

"Philip..."

"No!"

Miss Gloria just can't find the strength to argue. "Well, fine. Have it your way. You is a big man anyway and Lord knows..." She slam the door shut, lock it.

That's how it started. He would sleep outdoors some nights, walk the streets, make friends with the stars and the big like moon, hanging there like a calabash lamp in the sky.

7.

At first it would scare people a little, make them heart skip a beat, when they first look out on the water and see this woman floating, her untidy locks spread out behind her like Medusa, her face as expressionless as formica. But they get used to it.

Nobody was going to call police on her, but Floating Mary started to break into Goodpeople's yards. Only reason rottweiler and doberman didn't bite her up is because they was too stunned when they see this woman, brazen as all hell, scaling fence and walking past them like nothing. And also, they couldn't smell any fear in her.

So in the morning, Goodpeople would wake up and find this dirty woman floating in their swimming pools. They called police. Police came to haul her ass to jail. Between the water and the strong hands pulling her out, Mary shouting, "I have been poured out like water!"

Eh! Who would have thought that for her twenty-three years of sanity she had tried desperately to write poems but just couldn't do it. Now, when she speak, the red words tumble out like something straight from the Psalms.

8.

Is little white patches they attach to Mary's head. The patches were attached to thin wires, and the wires to an electric source; as if this kind of therapy could fix Mary's brain. Who tell them water and electricity could mix? It only fixing her from going into Goodpeople's swimming pool. It only stopping her from floating.

9.

He found the huge calabash tree growing in an open lot. It wasn't far from his house. This is where Philip now spent his days and even some of his nights. He loved the shade of the tree. He liked watching the green fruits for weeks, how they would swell up so big; how, eventually, their green skins would seem to turn into wood.

Sometimes he would yank one off the tree and shake it. It never sounded like his rattles. In fact, it never sounded at all. But he could feel the water moving inside it. Pure water. Water without boundaries or walls. Is like it was a perfect world inside that calabash.

And is because it was so perfect inside he liked to break them, liked smashing them against a rock and watching the river flow out.

10.

Listen to another myth: some people say if the world is really a calabash and God holds it in his hands, then every evening he gets clumsy and drops it. At that moment, we all bleed a little. The red on the horizon is the gathering of our blood.

11.

They finally let Mary out and she start to walk the streets. Electric and water currents bouncing in her head make her twitch with every move. "Twitching Mary", that's what they call her now. Twitching Mary walking down Old Hope Road begging for ten cents or a dollar if you can afford it. Begging for a patty and a cocoa bread. Begging for someone to explain to her please, why men must be so evil, why a man would promise you the heavens and then just leave you so, leave you for another bigbottom woman.

Twitching Mary walking up Lady Musgrave Road through New Kingston straight 'cross into Barbican. Twitching Mary walking around Kingston, begging. That's how she come across Philip under the gourd tree.

When she see what he was doing, picking the calabashes and smashing them on the floor, things start make sense. She see how out of pure idleness a man could break a world. Without any conscious intention, she found herself running towards him. And, without announcing themselves, tears had finally risen up behind her eyes and were now falling out.

12.

Philip frighten to see this woman running to him.

"No! Stop it!" she was screaming, her mouth all full and angry with commands just like his mother, just like Miss Gloria. "Nonoonoooonooonooostopit!"

So why people always telling him to stop? What damn rules him always breaking? He held the big, brown calabash in his hand, high up in the air, ready to smash it down like an idiot-god.

"No! Please!" She reached him, fell to her knees, face to the ground, her locks brushing his feet. "Please."

Philip don't know what to do. Him standing up looking both dignified and clumsy, the calabash swaying above his head. Him face fall into a frown, the gourd slip from him hands, bounce on the tree roots and then stop against a rock.

It didn't break bad. Just a little crack – just a little water dripping out. Mary scrambled over, picked it up, cradled it in her arms. Perhaps she was still a little bit mad and is that make her push the calabash up underneath her shirt, against her stomach – making her look more than nine months pregnant – water coming down her thighs – as if she was ready, right then and there, to give birth to another broken world.

And who knows what Philip was still wanting, needing. But in Mary's newly pregnant state, he saw something, walked over timidly and rested his head against her belly.

13.

They say, in this world we are all splinters searching for our other parts, our unbroken selves.

This Dance

This dance, this dance, this dance is a war dance.
Sunday School song

"See it here. This is the house!"

*

This is the house.

This is really the house.

This is him, Jeremy Howell, parked up by the sidewalk, behind a long line of cars leading up to the house. Sitting behind the steering wheel, dressed-to-puss-backfoot, almost ready to dance. But it not so easy. Him thinking 'bout the law. The law which just two semesters ago him start to study. And him thinking about long time heroes like Quashie. Him have a drawing of Quashie in his bedroom, 'cause he been studying that hero from he was young. Quashie stand up to Buckra and break the law. And Jeremy thinking, tonight more than any night, him need to summon that kind of courage. But things is not so easy.

First him have to take in the shock. Breathe in, breathe out. Him not even on the inside of the house yet, but coming just this far could make anyone piss themself. Raaas! Is only a year ago him find out this place even exist, and look on him now. Him is really here. At the house.

Years ago, him used to go to a dance every Saturday night in August Town. In a yard surrounded by zinc, the speaker boxes so loud that the galvanized sheets fencing the property would be pulsing, as if each one had its own lungs and heart and blood vessels. And the zinc would hold on to the riddim – that doop-doop dooop-du-dooooop! A sound that is almost like a

151

heartbeat but not quite. A modified heartbeat, a souped-up heartbeat with spoiler and rims and speakers in the trunk. Almost a heartbeat but not quite – but enough so it can get inside you.

In August Town, Jeremy would find a girl to hold on to. Always the one with the strong back, the wire waist, the foot movements, he could hold on, and wine down low low low low. Take the woman to the ground with him. And people used to say, "Lawwd, that yout' can dance eeeeh."

But that wasn't his dance.

Wasn't it.

Almost his dance, but not quite.

The first time he ever paid attention to this house was a year ago when Kevin drove him up here. It was midday on a Saturday and nothing was going on; just a big quiet house surrounded by a concrete wall and tall black gates. Kevin stopped the car, smiled and said, "This is where them things happen. See it here. This is the house."

Tonight, a year later, Jeremy is almost ready, but it not so easy. Him thinking about the law. Him thinking about Quashie. Him thinking about this thing his Aunt Patsy keep on telling him, "I not afraid to dance..." But then him also think about his mother. What would his mother say if she knew he was at a place like this? She would hold her head and say "JesasSaviourPilotMe! Is what happen to you bwoy? Is what really happen to you?"

*

His mother sat him down one day, and told him serious, serious, that he was born with riddim in his bones. It ran in the family – sickle cell, hypertension and riddim in the bones, deep in the marrow where scientists say blood cells are formed. Hereditary. Riddim. Bones. As if by playing the right tune in the centre of the family graveyard, all hell would break loose, generations of skeletons rising up from out of the earth to dance and to shake their fleshless legs.

Well, sickle cell can kill you. Hypertension can kill you. Riddim in the bones can kill as bad as the worst of them. So he tries to be careful. Afraid of dancing in a way that would make him lose himself. It happen before... his Aunt Patsy lose herself dancing. "Lose herself completely! Clean out of her mind she gone. Give up her good good job", was what his mother said, which was not really fair because Aunt Patsy had a good enough job and even helped his mother out when things were tight. "Mad mad mad! That woman mad. Lef' her good life a foreign, come kotch up back in Jamaica!" which was not fair for his mother to say. Patsy wasn't kotching nowhere. She had her own house. But the real thing about it, as far as his mother saw things, was her return. That she came down to visit, and ended up staying. Mad! Mad as shad.

His mother and Aunt Patsy never really knew each other growing up. Half-sisters. Patsy, the product of a married man's gallivanting. They grew in different houses, each mother hating the other, and before Patsy was even a teenager, she was packed up and carried off to the States.

Twenty-four years later, when the gallivanting father died, it was only politeness that made Monica send a telegram to the sister she never knew. Who could have expected Patsy to come? Not even Patsy herself! Is really her husband see the telegram and insisted. "Honey," he said to her. "You've never been back. It'll be good for you. And for Pascal", talking 'bout their mulatto child, "she should know where her mother comes from. She should know about that side of her," meaning the "black" side. "I insist." That is how Patsy end up back in Jamaica. And worse than that, one Saturday evening, she ended up on a Jamaican bus.

Is like she did forget, or maybe she just never know, that a Kingston to St Ann bus is no place for a stuck-up-somebody like her to travel, no place for someone who malice Jamaica to travel. But there she was, she and her daughter, squeezed into a seat on a country bus. All around them market women smelling of pimento and sweat, smelling of mangoes and sweat, lime and sweat, banana and sweat; all these market women on their way home, chatting. Chatting so much that Patsy closed her eyes tight. As if that would block out the sound. But she was swaying on the riddim of their talk, and after a while she really did drift off to sleep.

She woke up half hour later because a Rastaman she never noticed before had started playing his drum. Rubbing his thumb across the goat skin – *woooooooooooh*, beating a riddim, *ka-dap, ka-dap, ka-da-da-da-da-dap*! And now the whole bus felt full up of this drumbeat. It was there behind the market women's talk, there behind the bob of their heads. It had seeped into the torn seats, into the unsold fruits, into the driver's driving – that riddim, almost like a heartbeat. And now her daughter, Pascal – almost five years old and suddenly learning about "that" side of her, the black side – was straining her neck, looking behind with bright eyes on the drummer, clapping her little hands to the beat. It made Patsy's temper start to boil. She reached over, clasped Pascal's hands and said dangerously, "Stop."

In all fairness, the little girl did try to stop. But the riddim was all over the bus. And you can't just ignore riddim. So now that she was keeping her hands still, her little feet, on their own accord, started to feel out the beat, swinging out then back in against the seat, *ka-dap, ka-dap, ka-dap*!

Something broke inside Patsy. She stood up in the bus and started one piece of shouting, "Stop it! Stop it! Staaap it!!" But even as she was shouting, she was shouting in time to the beat. Even as she trying to hold on to something, anything, she felt the walls inside her mashing up and the only thing she ended up holding was the riddim in her feet.

Is like she did forget, or maybe she just never know, Jamaica is no place for people who don't like Jamaica. The island can break down that hatred without you even notice. All too easy, you have fallen in love with the place.

You ever seen Revival? Real Zion 69 Hallelujah speak-in-tongues rabbasetiboshi Jamaican Revival? Patsy started to trump. Right leg forward, right leg back. Her fists clenched, her hands going round in a rolling motion, a digging motion. Getting into spirit. And is she same one, standing up there as if she could have ever gotten the riddim to stop, is she same one who finally raised the chorus:

> *I want a Revival in my soul*
> *I want a Revival in my soul*
> *I must apply to de blood of Jeeesus*
> *To get a Revival in my soul.*

And in the back of her mind she thinking, *But look at this, I come back home.* Patsy. Singing Revival, dancing Revival. And that's how she ended up staying. She sent Pascal back, but she herself never returned to the United States.

Mad! Mad as shad! Dance and lose herself. Give up her family. What a disgrace. That's what Jeremy's mother kept on saying. But Aunt Patsy, who had the patience of Job and bore the constant neh-neh-neh of her half-sister, would lean over to her nephew and explain, "Sometimes you have to lose yourself to find yourself. Sometimes what you most scared of, is what you been needing all along. I not afraid to dance my dance again."

And is those words exactly which bring Jeremy here. To the

house, the place he is most afraid of, and the place where he most wants to be.

He remembers that Saturday a year ago when Kevin drove him up here. In the middle of the day. No whole-heap of cars parked up on the outside. No music pumping. No dancing going on on the inside. No party was keeping. Kevin only point it out to say that whenever party *did* keep, is here it was kept. Jeremy looking on the house with these big eyes. Him so frighten to see that what he always take as make-up story – rumour, propaganda – was really so. That there was a place in Jamaica where other kinds of people gathered. People he would call nasty. Sodomites. Abomination. Jeremy spit out on the floor and ask, "This is really where them come?"

The question hurt Kevin who had only been trying to help. To show him that a space existed where him could dance his own dance. The question hurt, so Kevin answered bitterly, "Yes. This is where we meet."

Only then, Jeremy get to thinking about the word, "Them". They. Those. Over There. Trying to separate himself. But tonight, a year later, he was here, at the house. This is really the house. Raaas! He. Himself. Here!

*

That day, a year ago, when he was looking with his big eyes on this house way up in the hills, a secret kind of a place where people come to dance their unlawful dance, he remembered the history lessons he had done in school. His mind run on every slave, every Nanny and every Quashie who ran up into the mountains – *from whence does my help come from* – following the *ka-doooom ka-di-pa-da-da doooop*, following the sound through the darkness and through the trees, following it in order to dance. So they could lose themselves. So they could find themselves.

When he was in high school, he was in the debating club

and in the history club and in key club, young and full of the kind of politics that had in it more heart than brains. He used to look up on the hills, on the sudden territories of concrete, all those gigantic houses built on the hillside, and would say to himself mournfully, *Look how the hills losing their culture.* He saw the mountains as a place where rebellions happened, where they were hatched, fought and won. Though, what kind of a rebellion is it when people only fighting to be themselves?

But here him is in the mountains, outside the gate of a house. To go inside is rebellion, and to go inside is to be himself. Him thinking of Quashie who lost four of his toes. For seventeen years Quashie was held as property, lived worse than Buckra dog on Buckra plantation; he got all of three thousand, four hundred and ninety eight strokes from the whip, sixteen dog bites, three hundred days (when you count it all up) locked up in a room without windows. Seventeen years, and all that punishment for insubordination. For uppitiness. For his refusal to speak like a good ignorant nigger, for speaking the first language him ever know. All this punishment because he was a man with his own mind.

The first time Quashie try to run away, the dogs catch him by the heels and he was flogged. The second time, they take up the cutlass and cut off two toes from each foot, and even while him was bleeding, they leave him with a stern warning, "Next time, Boy, we'll cut everything below yer knee!"

That could not stop Quashie. A third time, he would try to make it to the mountains; and more than try, he would really make it. Drawn to the *ka-doooom ka-di-pa-da-da dooooop!* Drawn to the *ka-dap, ka-dap, ka-da-da-da-da-dap.* Drawn to the *doop-doop doooop-du-dooooop!* Quashie was a man born inside of Africa. Born with Africa inside of him. Africa in his bones, like a riddim.

*

This is the house. This is really the house. And inside the house, is his people. Inside is a place where him can dance the dance him did always want to dance. With the kind of people, the kind of man he has always wanted to dance with. A true true dance this time. From the inside out. It take bravery to do that. Strength.

And right then, even before he was done making his mind up fully, Jeremy's eyes started to water. Even before he turned on the engine and turned the car around, he had to hold his face tight so as not to make the eye-water spill. Because he knew he wasn't yet a man like Quashie. Not tonight. Him was not ready. Dressed-to-puss-backfoot, his black square shoes shined and a riddim playing in his head. He couldn't do it.

He would drive home instead. Maybe he would go over to Tia, his girlfriend, and rest his head in her lap. And when she asked, "What happen to you?" he would tell her, "Nothing."

"No, is not nothing. You always have these times when you get into this mood. Like I can't reach you."

"I know. I sorry. Is just... is just..." And what could he tell her? That sometimes she was all he needed, but another time she was like plantation whips and missing toes and punishment? No man can tell him girl those things, and some men in this island will never dance the way they want to dance.

So even as him driving down the hill, away from the house, away from defiance and rebellion, he had to swallow hard, him face still tight from holding the tears. A riddim playing somewhere in his head, the volume turned down low.